I0617788

15 Serial Killers

Docufictions
by Harold Jaffe

Visuals by Joel Lipman

Copyright © 2003 by Harold Jaffe
All rights reserved

Published by Raw Dog Screaming Press
Hyattsville, MD

First printing 2003

Cover image: Andi Olsen
Interior illustrations: Joel Lipman
Book design: Jennifer C. Barnes
Author photo: Gayle Luque

Printed in the United States of America

ISBN 0-9745031-0-X

Library of Congress Control Number: 2003096904

www.rawdogscreaming.com

Critical Response to Harold Jaffe's Fiction

False Positive
"These short treats transform 15 news vignettes into gruesomely interesting oddities...Jaffe is a master at illuminating our culture's most evasive grotesqueries." —San Francisco Chronicle

Sex for the Millennium
"Something's going on here, low-key, cool, and disturbing. These subtle displacements of desire fix to your memory, and, with their humor and pathos, gnaw there a long time." —Samuel R. Delany

Straight Razor
"As technically outrageous and emotionally intense as a madman's shotgun held to the temple of contemporary culture. [Jaffe's 12 stories] succeed terrifically." —Review of Contemporary Fiction

Othello Blues
"Composed almost wholly of stage directions, quick cuts, and dialogue, Jaffe's novel is an imaginative, witty, and politically prescient retelling of Othello." —Thomas LeClair

Eros Anti-Eros
"Jaffe's fictions are a wonder of deadpan humor, biting wit, and visual beauty. No recent fiction has gripped me with such force and immediacy. —Marianne Hauser

Madonna and Other Spectacles
"Crackling with rage and black laughter, these fictions wrench themselves out of the grimmest facts: genocide, nuclear devastation, black poverty, corporate murder. [This is] a collection that confronts terror in street lannguage and redoubles its impact." —Publisher's Weekly

Beasts
"Jaffe's convincing portraits of the dispossessed are moving, insightful glimpses of the human spirit under stress." —The New York Times Book Review

Dos Indios
"Told with the simplicity of a folk tale, this spiritual journey of a Peruvian flute player is a beautiful and moving story." —Newsday

Books by Harold Jaffe

15 Serial Killers (docufictions; visuals by Joel Lipman)
False Positive (fictions)
Sex for the Millennium (extreme tales)
Straight Razor (stories; visuals by Norman Conquest)
Othello Blues (novel)
Eros Anti-Eros (fictions)
Madonna and Other Spectacles (fictions)
Beasts (fictions)
Dos Indios (novel)
Mourning Crazy Horse (stories)
Mole's Pity (novel)

Acknowledgements

A number of these "docufictions" were published in the following journals and anthologies: *Submodern*; *Obscure Publications*; *Denver Quarterly*; *Journal of Experimental Fiction*; *Sick: An Anthology of Illness*; *The Dream People*; *Trystero* (Germany); *Kung Avantzine* (Italy); *Fiction International*.

I'd like to thank Stephen-Paul Martin and Gayle Luque for reading and commenting on this volume in manuscript.

Contents

Dahmer 11

Clown 22

Son of Sam 31

Wuornos 46

Big Ed 59

Dr. K 72

Dr. Death .81

Night Stalker 94

Lonely Hearts 106

Slick Ted .116

Starkweather 127

K & K 135

Speck 143

Carlos the Jackal 151

Manson 161

For G.L.

Only at the extremes is there freedom

—Georges Bataille

⊕Dahmer⊖

Konerak Sinthasomphone

What are the Milwaukee cops supposed do with a name like that?
Flattened nose, coarse black hair, slanted lidless eyes.
Adolescent? Granddaddy? No way to tell with orientals.
Wednesday, April 17, 1991, 2:20 a.m.
Raunchy, high-crime, inner city sector near Marquette University.
Konerak Sinthasomphone, 14, small, naked, bruised and bloody, is running for his life.
But he's not screaming, not making a sound.
The oriental tends to be silent or hysterically noisy, rarely in between.
A young black woman, Harriet Cross, sees the naked panicked boy from her third story window and dials 911.
The paramedics get to him first, cover his nakedness with a blanket.
Rousted from the all-night donut shop, the police pull up in their patrol car.
Biceps, Beretta 9 mm's, disabling gasses, billy clubs.
Here they call them Tyrone clubs because the cops are always whacking black folks.
The miniature Asian is squatting silently on the pavement in a blanket beside the paramedic van.
He seems to be trembling.
On one side is Harriet Cross and her mother Luella Cleveland.
On the other side is a tall, stiff, 30-ish white man with dirty blond hair.

Jeffrey Dahmer.

In his deceptively calm manner, Dahmer is explaining to the cops that Konerak is his 18-year-old lover who swallowed too much sweet wine and fell on his face.

Harriet Cross and Luella Cleveland protest that the Asian boy was trying to resist the blond man who was punching and kicking him up and down the street.

The cops have got to make a decision.

The tall stiff white dude is an identifiable homo that sexes with colored orientals.

A combo any righteous cop's gonna hate from his heart.

But the other two are mouthy black females.

No contest; the females are told to go home.

Then the two cops in their thick black shoes escort the blanketed oriental and tall white fag to Dahmer's one bedroom apartment on the second floor of 924 North 25th Street, the Oxford Apartments.

The apartment smells funny but is neat.

Homos tend to be neat.

The oriental kid's clothes are draped over a chair.

Two Polaroid photos of the boy in his paisley bikini underwear are tacked to the wall above the sofa.

Konerak puts on his pants and shirt that were on the chair, then sits on the edge of the sofa, still mute.

Dahmer is sweet-talking, promising that future lovers' spats will not spill over on to the street.

The cops yawn. They're getting hungry.

They nod and leave the 14-year-old Laotian boy with Jeffrey Dahmer. Case closed.

Had the Milwaukee cops glanced into the bedroom they would have found the decomposing remains of a 17-year-old black teen named Clarence McKee.

The police have scarcely left the Oxford Apartments when Dahmer strangles Konerak Sinthasomphone.

Scarcely settled their thick rumps into the patrol car when Dahmer anally sodomizes the corpse.

He beheads the corpse and boils the head.

Fits the skinned head into the freezer alongside the other heads.

Dissects the body, excising the genitals which he puts into a large jar of formaldehyde filled with genitals.

Ambrosia Chocolate

Jeffrey Dahmer moves from his grandmother's house in West Allis, Wisconsin to the Oxford Apartments in Milwaukee on September 25, 1988.

By then he's killed and dismembered at least four young men and boys.

Modus operandi: hit on a mark at a gay bar or bathhouse and offer him $$ to come back to Dahmer's grandmother's house and pose for Polaroids.

Once in his grandmother's basement Dahmer drugs the mark's drink, strangles him with his hands or his old army belt, orally and/or anally sodomizes the corpse, dismembers it.

Depending on his mood, he will cannibalize the corpse, sever a bicep, say, deep fry it in Crisco.

The cannibalization becomes a regular occurrence as the murders multiply.

The day after moving into the Oxford Apartments, Dahmer accosts a 13-year-old Laotian boy and offers him $25 to pose for Polaroids.

He dopes the boy's diet Pepsi and anally rapes him.

Then, for reasons unknown, Dahmer releases him.

The 13-year-old Laotian's name is Saravane Sinthasomphone, by coincidence, the older brother of Konerak Sinthasomphone, whom Dahmer will murder in 1991.

Saravane reports the incident to his parents who take him to the emergency room.

After a seven-hour wait, it is confirmed that he's been drugged and anally raped.

The police arrest Dahmer at the Ambrosia Chocolate factory where he works as a "mixer," presumably while wearing latex gloves and a hairnet.

The charge is sexual exploitation of a child and second-degree sexual assault.

Dahmer pleads guilty but insists that the boy said he was 19.

While awaiting sentence, Dahmer picks up a 22-year-old black male named Harvey Shammgod at a gay bathhouse, offers him money to model, brings him back to his apartment on 924 North 25th Street, drugs him, strangles him, sodomizes then cannibalizes his corpse.

Harvey Shammgod's death is either not reported or reported but not logged by the police.

At his sentencing Dahmer, on trial for sexual assault, has now murdered at least five young males.

He speaks on his own behalf, blames his assault of the Laotian boy on his alcoholism, vows to turn his life around, promises to enroll in AA.

It is, as these things go, a smooth performance.

The old white judge buys it and gives Dahmer a suspended sentence.

Interestingly, Dahmer's father, Lionel, writes to the court pleading that his son not be released until he receives psychiatric treatment.

Lionel Dahmer's plea is set aside.

Two days after his release on January 16, 1989, Jeffrey Dahmer kills again.

In the next fourteen months he will savage and murder twelve more young men and boys.

Sex Slave

By now Dahmer has the drill down.

Accost the mark at a bar or bathhouse, lure him back to the Oxford Apartments by promising him money to pose or inviting him to drink beer and watch pornographic videos.

Drug the mark by adding pulverized prescription sleeping pills to his drink.

Strangle the mark, sodomize, dismember and cannibalize the corpse.

Masturbate while handling the warm, stinking, rainbow-colored viscera of the cut-open body.

After stripping the edible portions and severing the head and genitals, dispose of the corpse.

The skinned heads store in the freezer, the genitalia in large jars of formaldehyde, the strips of edible flesh wrapped in tin foil in the fridge.

Experiment with spices and tenderizers to make the flesh more palatable.

Experiment with various methods of disposing of the corpse: potent acids, chemical mixtures that reduce flesh, bone and viscera to slime.

Flush the residue down the toilet.

If the residue is lumpy or bony, dump it into a sewer outside.

One novelty Dahmer hits upon is drilling a hole in the victim's skull while he is drugged but alive.

Filling the vacuum with hydrochloric acid.

The idea is to turn the victim into a kind of zombie or sex slave that will do Dahmer's bidding absolutely.

That initiative leads nowhere.

And if someone discovers the beheaded heads?

Dahmer paints them grey to imitate plastic lab models.

What about his neighbors in the Oxford Apartments?

The drilling, the agonizing shrieks, the stench of chemicals and decomposition?

The neighbors are mostly working-class African-Americans who evidently are more tolerant of eccentricity than other humans.

In truth Dahmer does not take strict measures to prevent getting caught.

He is caught when a mark, Reginald Edwards, 20, escapes from Dahmer's clutches with one handcuff dangling from his wrist.

The young black man leads the skeptical cops back to Dahmer's apartment.

Dahmer, rational, composed, launches into his explanation, even displaying the key to the handcuffs.

One of the cops shuffles into the bedroom to have a look and, in a trembling voice, shouts to his partner.

"Vince, cuff the son of a bitch."

When Dahmer hears those fateful words he starts to flail and kick.

After he's bitch-slapped and cuffed, the cops have a closer look around.

Skinned heads in the freezer.

Strips of flesh in the fridge.

Genitals in large jars of formaldehyde.

Bits of bone and cartilage under foot.

The sweet-sour stench of decomposition.

Once Upon a Time

Even a same-sex, serial killing, cannibalistic necrophile has a life.

What I'm trying to say is that every narrative, no matter how squalid, must have its genesis.

Jeffrey Lloyd Dahmer was born on May 21, 1960, in Milwaukee, Wisconsin, the Badger state.

Lionel, his father, was a research chemist with a Ph.D.

Joyce, his mother, was a substitute high school typing and short-hand teacher.

By all accounts infant Jeffrey was a bubbly child.

He loved animals, both real and stuffed, and was crazy about his miniature Dachshund, Pipi.

An early incident recalled by Lionel Dahmer in his memoir *A Father's Story* is of the three of them: he, his wife Joyce, and four-year-old Jeffrey nursing a baby robin that injured a wing when it had flown into a window.

Jeffrey cradled the trembling creature in his small hands, then released it into the air.

The robin hovered briefly then flew strongly up and away.

It was a moment, the father recounted, of a simple but powerful sharing which would never be duplicated.

Lionel Dahmer claims that a change came over young Jeffrey after his surgery for a double hernia.

At age six the child suddenly lost his ebullience.

Instead of growing up he seemed to be growing in, inward.

He became uncommunicative yet somehow fragile.

He would sit for hours motionless staring at nothing.

Dahmer senior attributes the change to all the moving the family was doing.

Nor did Jeffrey have a sibling to share the anxiety since his brother David was not yet born.

Because he was completing his doctorate at Iowa State, Lionel Dahmer moved the family in a matter of months from Milwaukee to Ames, Iowa, to Akron, Ohio, where he landed a job as a research chemist.

Jeffrey must have felt as if his moorings were cut loose.

At the same time, Lionel and Joyce were having marital problems.

In Akron, the introverted Lionel spent long hours at his job, while high-strung Joyce, pregnant with David, would talk on the phone or watch TV.

Child Jeffrey was largely left to his own devices.

In his memoir Lionel recounts a disturbing incident which attests to young Jeffrey's growing estrangement.

Once, when Jeff was seven, Lionel crawled under the wood framehouse and dislodged some animal bones that had been rattling at night.

Evidently, a badger had killed possums, rats and mice, feasting on them under the house.

When Jeffrey saw the pile of animal bones his father had swept into the yard, a strange smile appeared on his face.

In Lionel's words, the child's "small hands dug deep into the pile of bones. He seemed oddly thrilled by the sound they made. I can no longer view it simply as a childish episode, a passing fascination. This sense of something dark and shadowy, of a malicious force growing in my son, now colors almost every memory."

As an adolescent Jeffrey would collect road kill, put the remains in a trash bag, then skin and stroke the smashed, bloody creatures.

Once he mounted the head of a large possum on a stick and thrust it into the ground next to his mother's clothesline.

As a teenager, Jeff seemed devoid of normal interests.

Not sports, not girls, not academic goals, not boyhood friendships.

Lionel speculates that his son's inexpressible fascination with decomposition and death had already encircled him.

That the boy knew there was no one to whom he could unburden himself.

After doing poorly in high school then flunking out of Ohio State after a single semester of almost constant drunkenness, Jeff returned home to his now divorced father in Akron in Spring '79.

Dahmer senior convinced his son to enlist in the army.

Stationed in Fort Leonard Wood, Missouri as a combat engineer, Dahmer got into fights with bunkmates toward whom he'd made indecent advances.

After basic training his company was shipped to Düsseldorf, Germany.

Among the Aryans, Dahmer seems to have really cut loose, drinking heavily, going AWOL, sexually accosting other servicemen.

During his time in Düsseldorf there was a series of unsolved murders of young males.

When Dahmer was arrested in the US a dozen years later the German authorities mounted a retrospective investigation but came up empty.

Dahmer was dishonorably discharged from the army in 1980 for fighting, absence without leave, and "habitual drunkenness."

Lawyers Lawyers

The selection of jurors for the much ballyhooed Dahmer trial in Milwaukee generated bitterness in the black community.

Though thirteen of Dahmer's seventeen known murder victims were black, the jury was composed of six males and six females, all white.

Gerald Boyle, Dahmer's attorney, had his client plead guilty by reason of insanity.

Then Boyle unrolled the filthy, bloody bandage of Dahmer's perversions, mutilations, murders, necrophilia and cannibalization.

Boyle's contention was that only a certified madman would commit such atrocities.

That Dahmer should be placed in an institution for the criminally insane rather than imprisoned for life.

Rick McCann, the deputy DA, employed many of the same examples to convince the jurors that Dahmer was a psychopath and manipulator who must bear full responsibility for his heinous crimes.

Why else, McCann asked rhetorically, would Dahmer deliberately suspend murdering at certain periods, as when he was in the army or at college.

Indisputably, Dahmer was fully in control of his actions.

Defense counsel Boyle labeled his client a "runaway train."

Deputy DA McCann called him the "evil engineer."

The jury in its wisdom decided for McCann.

Dahmer, found guilty and responsible for his fatal deviations, was sentenced to seventeen consecutive life terms.

Malcolm 2X Scarver

At Columbia Institute in Portage, Wisconsin, Jeffrey Dahmer was kept in isolation.

He was a model prisoner.

After nearly two years the prison authorities permitted Dahmer, at his request, to have restricted contact with other inmates.

On the morning of November 28, 1994, Dahmer, multiple murderer of young black males, was assigned to a detail of three for latrine cleanup.

One of the others, a white named Jesse Anderson, had murdered his wife and blamed it on a black intruder.

The third was a fiercely violent, schizophrenic black nationalist named Malcolm 2X Scarver.

The escorting guard, according to his testimony, left the three alone for less than fifteen minutes.

When he returned he found the two white inmates murdered, Anderson's skull crushed, Dahmer's throat slashed, the blood squirting, his neck almost unhinged.

The bloody, razor-sharp knife, fashioned out of a soup spoon, lay on the cement floor next to the near-decapitated Dahmer.

Their executioner, Malcolm 2X Scarver?

He was, the escorting guard would testify, diligently mopping the latrine area while whistling.

What was he whistling?

The guard admitted to having a poor ear for music but thought it might have been that Sinatra favorite: "My Way."

⊙ Clown ⊙

Gacy? I thought you said Bundy.

They nailed Gacy's fat butt in '78.

Got himself 21 life sentences and 12 death sentences.

You know what? He deserved every bit of it.

Executed by lethal injection on May 10, 1994 in Stateville Correctional Center, Joliet, Illinois.

Ring a bell?

Same joint where mass murderer Richard Speck would drop dead of a heart attack in '91.

Speck was a YY dummy who raped then snuffed a bunch of nurses.

That was in '66.

Maybe it was snuff then rape, I don't know.

Speck ended up in pink silk drawers with hormone-induced titties wagging his coated tongue like a bitch in heat.

Gacy was no YY.

John Wayne Gacy was more puke than Duke, a half-ass male from the get-go.

Before zapping him they asked him if he had any final words.

"Yeah, I do. Kiss my ass."

Exit scumbag.

Every exit must have an entrance, right?

Gacy's mom died when he was nine.

Or maybe she didn't die then but was so passive that she might as well have.

His abusive dad was an obsessively macho, borderline psychotic booze-hound.

He called John "Jock" to mock the boy's delicate constitution.

Gacy, a Pisces, got married at 22 to still his own doubts about adequacy.

Became a proud and successful manager of a Kentucky Fried Chicken franchise in Waterloo, Iowa.

Upstanding member of the Junior Chamber of Commerce.

Honorary Secretary of the Waterloo chapter of Freemasons.

Yo, nothing that good lasts forever.

With two kids of his own, Gacy withdrew his libido from Lucille, his wife, and pursued adolescent boys.

Lucille is also the name of BB King's guitar.

Reckon I ought to introduce myself: My name is Rob.

My mother's name is Roberta.

We come from Roboland.

And we sell rotisseries.

My friends call me Hungsolo.

Gacy called me Hung.

I called him Neck, as in redneck.

Though redneck really didn't do him justice.

I should say here that I ain't a groupie and I ain't a homey.

And you got to know I ain't no homo.

Let's just say I'm captivated by extremity.

Plus I have the cream to pursue my dream.

Made the big $$$ in real estate, same as with Neck.

That's about it as far as what we have in common.

Case you were wondering.

Before prisoner Gacy permitted a visitor he had the wannabe fill out a strict questionnaire.

I wrote I was an ex-lawyer-turned-writer who wanted to recount John Wayne Gacy's story from his own eyes.

Gacy bought the lie.

But what got his juices flowing was my writing I was hung like a horse.

I visited Neck Gacy six times for a total of 23 hours in 1993 and '94 at Menard Correctional Center in Chester, Illinois.

Neck also phoned, faxed and e-mailed me at least a hundred times.

I kept vids, tapes or written records of all of it.

We were tight.

Only he thought we were tighter than I did.

I had severe misgivings about the guy.

Like most serial murderers (mass murderers are different), Neck was a born liar, real slick at it even though he was lumpy and unappealing from a physical standpoint.

The first time I saw him in February 18, 1993 I was struck at how ordinary he looked.

I don't know what I was expecting but he was definitely on the fat side.

About five-seven, 215, with a twisted, upturned nose, wide nostrils and large oily pores.

He had invisible eyebrows, limp colorless hair streaked with grey, two-and-a-half chins, and an infectious grin which made him enormously likeable.

Neck was 100 percent Irish with a hefty dose of blarney.

You can see how he charmed children and adults in or out of his Pogo the clown getup.

Hell, as the Jaycee's "Man of the Year," Neck maneuvered himself into a photo-op with the then First Lady, Rosalyn Carter, both of 'em wearing shit-eating grins.

This was in '77.

After the photo-op he banged her.

True story. Neck balled Rosalyn in the same Chicago suburb tract house where he'd sliced and diced young boys, sprinkled the corpses with quicklime, then lodged them in the crawl space beneath his porch.

Done twenty-five or thirty like that.

Happily, Rosalyn's sinuses were acting up and she couldn't smell the roses.

President Jimmy?

Off in the South Bronx retrofitting tenements in the barrio.

Teaching the poorest of the poor how to pull themselves up by their bootstraps.

I always felt Jimmy should have gotten the Nobel Peace Prize for the hands-on work he did with poor folks instead of Kissinger with his Strangelove posturings.

Here's some of what the cops found in Gacy's Chicago suburb tract house after they nabbed him in December '78 and dug up the bodily remains in the crawl space:

• Eleven porno movies made in Denmark.

• Porno books and magazines with titles such as: *Satan Says: Submit*; *The Naked and the Dead, by Norman Mailer*; *I Swallow*; *The Gay Guide to Minneapolis-St. Paul*; *Men Who Worship Boys*; *The Selected Musings of Gore Vidal*.

• Four hypodermic syringes.

• Six pairs of wrist and leg irons, with keys.

• A twenty foot section of heavy linked chain.

• Thirty-six Polaroid pictures of Pizzerias in the Chicago area.

• Eighteen various sized dildos and butt pugs, several with dried blood and fecal matter.

• A five-year-old wall calendar featuring Disney World in Orlando, Florida.

• Marijuana and rolling paper.

• A wall-mounted pencil sharpener

• Black rubber executioner's hoods, black leather strait jackets, padded rubber blindfolds, chain mail jock straps, and heavy duty Spandex piss gags.

• Two large Mason jars of Snickers and Almond Joy.

Flash forward to '93.

I was living in Omaha, Nebraska, a young and wealthy widower.

Down young bro' comin' straight out of 'Braska.

When visiting condemned killers it was my habit to take the same route and do the same things en route.

Call it ritual, superstition, whatever.

I'd sleep on my left side and in the morning have a bloody mary instead of the usual sectioned grapefruit.

Three-and-a-third spoons of sugar in my coffee instead of four.

Post-breakfast, I used Pepsodent rather than Sensodyne, which was a sacrifice because I have sensitive teeth and gums.

I wore Versace silk thong jocks rather than standard cotton jockeys or boxers.

When visiting the condemned, I traveled with two females, who varied but were always sultry.

Leave Saturday morning, fly my Piper from Omaha to St Louis, put up there at the Waterfront Hilton and party bigtime Saturday night, always ending with me, my fems, and a couple or three others, male and/or fem, sexing into the wee hours.

Followed by pizza and coffee.

The pizza had to have pepperoni, anchovies and pineapple, the other toppings didn't matter.

Followed by the jacuzzi.

Followed by sleep, the deep drugged sleep of the just.

The waitresses at brunch outside St. Louis would always ask where we were headed and when we told them John Wayne Gacy they would get like all hot and bothered.

Good girls and bad are into outlaws. Period.

Call yourself "Kid" and you'll get their attention.

I always reserved a 1993 silver and chocolate Mercedes for the two-and-a-half hour drive to Chester, Illinois.

Had a name for the Benz: Berkowitz. Private joke.

My two female companions were not morning people and were at each other's throats all the way to Chester.

I laughed so hard I peed my jocks.

I don't know about you but I love a cat fight.

Chester, Illinois?

Have you ever shined your brights on rats in a junkyard at two a.m. in the freezing rain?

Maybe take a pop at them with your 12-gauge?

That's Chester, Illinois.

Menard, on the banks of the Mississippi, is an old bleak, brick "correctional center."

You check your metal, get eyeballed, x-rayed, patted down, then meet with your inmate flesh to flesh, though he's cuffed of course.

My two fems would blow kisses at Neck but not go into the visiting area with us till I gave the sign.

I'd be lying if I said Neck didn't make a pass at me the first time he saw me.

He was cuffed, like I said.

We sat facing each other but with no partition.

He was wearing some kind of sweet cologne he must've put on for the occasion.

He tried to rub my bulge with his knee.

After I rebuffed him he grabbed me with his cuffed hands hard around the neck from behind and hissed into my ear:

"I could snap your neck, right now, Puss!"

I was surprised at the power in his arms.

Immediately, two guards burst in, but it was over.

Once Neck said it he seemed to forget it.

He was cool after that.

Well, as cool as John Wayne Gacy can be.

I always brought him stuff: Snickers, Almond Joy, art supplies.

In turn, he let the guards snap photos of him and me and the girls.

Sometimes he brought his newest clown paintings, which he either gave me or sold to me on the cheap.

Pogo the clown grinning in his harlequin garb facing the viewer.

Beneath the smears of bright color you could tell Pogo the clown

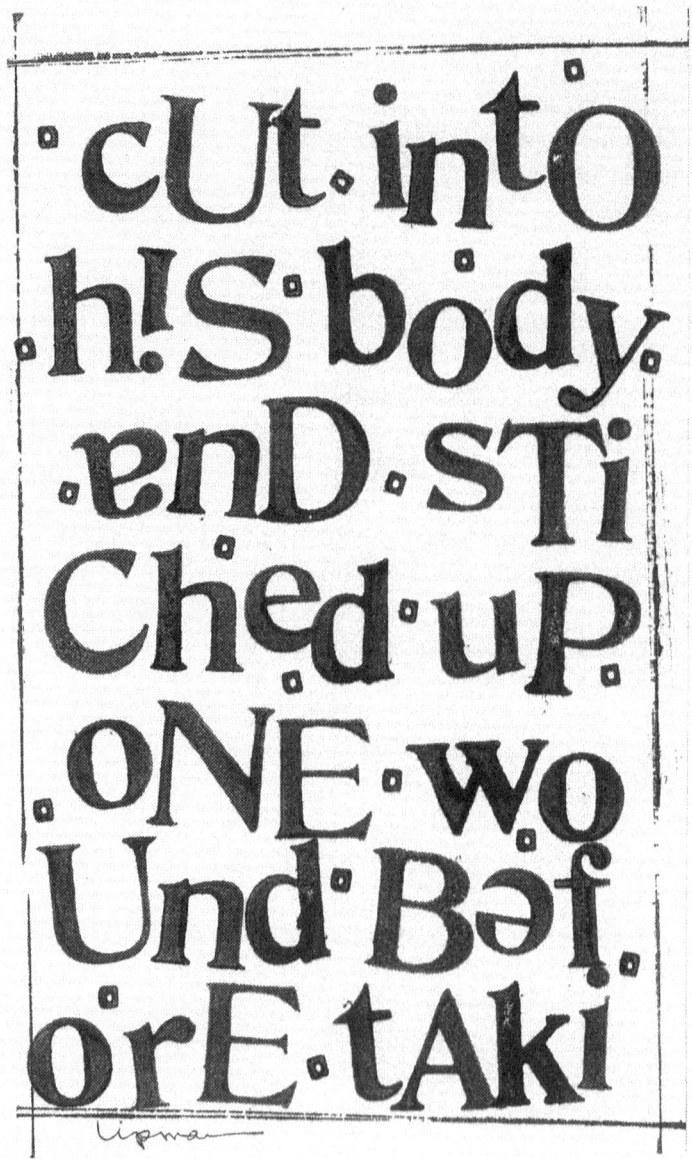

cUt intO
hiS body
aNd STi
Ched uP
oNE wo
Und Bef
orE tAki

was Gacy himself, his grin wide as a cut throat.

As art, the stuff sucked.

You know what: I resold a pair of clown paintings to a prestigious online gallery three or four months ago.

One was an oil, the other acrylic.

Genuine Gacy's.

Fetched me 41 thou.

For the most part Neck and me, we'd talk about ordinary things: home team sports, the nuclear family, encroachment of high technology, the increasing threat of terrorism from the Muslim sector.

Occasionally he turned the conversation to boys, but he'd always catch himself and change the subject.

Once I asked him: "So it gave you pleasure?", referring to 12-year-old Billy Carroll, handcuffed, tortured, sodomized, chloroformed, mutilated, then sprinkled with quicklime and buried in the crawl space.

"Doing Billy Carroll that way gave you pleasure, Neck?"

Neck looked at me hard from beneath his invisible eyebrows.

Then his mouth got all slack.

I couldn't tell if he was going to laugh or cry?

"What do you think?" he said.

What I thought was he was a despicable homo pederast mother-fucking piece of shit.

"I think you're presidential timber," I said.

"If you weren't here in Menard you'd be fartin' around in the Rose Garden.

"Setting policy for the greatest country in the fingerfuckin' free world, Neck."

It was a joke, but Neck didn't buy it.

Just sort of sat there with a weird expression on his face.

I said: "Neck, it's hard to get you to break a smile, but when you put on those Pogo the clown getups, you grin to beat the band.

"And then you go and paint your happy grinning clowns.

"How did you come up with the clown thing, Neck?"

He looked at my eyes to see if I was mocking him.

Finally he said: "I love folks, Hung.

"Specially young folks, adolescent boys and such.

"Love to see 'em happy."

By then it was pushing 4:00 pm, which meant we had to clear out. That was the law.

The last time I saw Neck alone was five days before his execution. Which wasn't in Menard but in Stateville, like I said.

I pointed to my bulge and let him run the back of his handcuffed hand over it.

Then I backed up and shook my head.

"No more cock.

"You've had it for this lifetime, Neck.

"Think about it in hell."

Those were the last words I said to him.

He phoned me the next morning, but I didn't take the call.

⊕Son of Sam⊖

Dear Captain Mitch O'Reilly:

I am deeply hurt by you calling me a wemon hater. I am not. What I am is a monster. I am the Son of Sam. I am a little brat.

When old man Sam gets drunk he gets evil. He beats his family. But he don't beat off. No sir. And sometimes he ties me to the back of the house. Or locks me in the garage. It smells real bad in there, Captain Mitch. Sam loves to drink blood.

"Go out and kill," commands Father Sam.

Behind our house they have their eternal rest. Young wemon, raped and slaughtered, blood drained—they're just bones now.

Papa Sam keeps me locked in the attic. I can't get out but I look out the attic window and watch the world go by. And what a disgusting sight it is. It's absolutely repulsive, Captain Mitch.

Me—I am an outsider. I'm on a different wave length than the rest of you Robo Sapiens. I am a murderer that admits to being a murderer. You say you want to stop me, Captain Mitch. Well, then, you must kill me. Attention all precinct houses and donut shops: Shoot first and question later. Empty your semi-automatics and riot shotguns into the Son of Sam. Papa Sam is real old,

Captain Mitch. He needs some blood to preserve his youth. He has had too many heart attacks. Too many farty infarctions. "Ach, me hoot. It hoits, sonny boy."

I miss my pretty wabbit most of all. She's resting in the ladies room. Imagine her sweet floppy ears. Have you ever heard a wabbit shriek in pain, Captain Mitch? It would melt your hard cop's heart. But I will see her soon because I am the monster— Beelzebub, the chubby behemoth.

I love to hunt, Captain Mitch. Blood sports. Prowling the streets of our great boroughs. Excluding Staten Island of course. I am looking for meat. The wemon of Queens are the prettiest of all. It must be the water they drink. I live for the hunt, it's my life. Blood for the old man, Papa Sam.

Captain Mitch, I don't want to kill anymore. No sir. But a respectable churchgoer like you realizes that I must "honor thy father." What I want to do is make love to the world. For that I will need more of that sticky white stuff, it's gooey but it's good. I will pump iron and increase my consumption of donuts, like your guys in blue do, New York City's finest.

I don't belong on earth, Captain Mitch. Return me to the yahoos. To the human beans of this great city, I proclaim my love. And I want to wish you all a happy Easter. For I will rise to see that the yahoos and the fine wemon of these boroughs have a long and peaceful sleep. Once all the blood is washed off.

Ach. Old man Sam is wheezing and barking. Time for me to haul ass.

Bye for now.
SOS

Burly, handsome, the son, grandson, and great-grandson of NYC police officers, forty-three-year-old Captain Mitch O'Reilly headed Operation Omega, the city-wide task force whose sole charge was: Apprehend the loon that was cold-bloodedly murdering females in various parts of the city with a .44 handgun at point blank range.

The killer, Son of Sam, as he called himself, had previously written to the well-known newspaper reporter-bon vivant, Jimmy Breslin. But this was the first time he'd contacted the police.

Was the letter as wacko as it seemed? Or was it intricately coded? The killer was obviously compelled to display his high IQ.

"Donuts" came up several times. And women, deliberately misspelled as "wemon." Also "yahoos" which evidently was a derogatory term used by Mets fans for the NY Yankees. Yahoos also appeared in his letter to Breslin, a rabid Yankee fan. Robo Sapiens was a pun of some kind, underlined to call attention to itself.

What about the rabbits with their floppy ears and pathetic shrieks? Doctor Myron C. Kessel, the police psychiatrist attached to the task force, interpreted the floppy ears as representing the killer's lack of self-esteem, and especially his inability to get an erection in normal ways. He needed to kill desirable young females in order to consummate his desire for them, which he did through masturbation. The "pathetic shrieks" represented the killer's agonizing impotence.

As far as the killer getting his orders from "father Sam," that could very well be a red herring to throw the police off his trail.

What it boiled down to was one of two theories: Either the killer was a psycho pure and simple, or he was faking madness to implement his bloody vendetta against females.

Dear Sam Carr:

I have asked you please and pretty please: Stop that dog of yours from howling all day and all night. Yet he continues to do so. I pleaded with you, Sam Carr. I told you how the barking

and wheezing and howling was destroying my digestion and my family. How the barking and howling would make me scream, scream out begging for the noise to stop. It never stopped.

Now I know what kind of a human bean you are and what kind of a family you are. You are cruel and inconsiderate. You have no love for any other human beans. You're selfish, Mr. Sam Carr. My life is destroyed now. I have nothing to lose anymore. I can see that there shall be no peace in my life or my family's life while you are still alive and farting.

I have called out the names of the masters: John Wheaties, General Jack Cosmo, The Womb Raider. Their verdict is unanimous: you are dead poo. I'll see you in hell, old Sam Carr.

Four days later, Carr heard a gunshot coming from the doghouse in his backyard where he discovered his beloved six-year-old black Labrador, Harvey, bleeding on his side on the ground. A heavy-set male wearing a yellow rain slicker, hightop black and white sneakers and and baseball cap was bounding away.

Harvey died in intensive care three-and-a-half hours later.

Carr reported the occurrence to the local Yonkers police and handed them the offending letter. The Yonkers police filed it under "Low Priority."

Dear Jake Cassara,

I'm sorry to hear about that fall you took from the roof of your house. And what happened to your groin. That's what you get from straddling the roof like it's a pony. It ain't a pony, Jake, it's just a freaking tract house, and you're a despicable couch potato.

Anyway, I just want to say I'm sorry. I'm sure it won't be long until you are on the mend. Please be careful next time since you're going to be confined for a very long time. You're going to be confined throughout all eternity, Jake. Where? Straight down and down, where the giant jackhammer goes, an airless place with a very bad smell. I think you'll like it.

Let us know if Jane needs anything from the meat slaughterer.

Yours truly,
Sam and Frances Carr

Jake Cassara had not fallen off his roof. And aside from BPH (benign prostate hypertrophy), his groin was intact. Nor had he ever met Sam and Frances Carr. His wife's name was Jean, not Jane. And he didn't have any acquaintances among meat slaughterers.

He dialed 411 to get the Carr's phone number from Information and phoned them; they agreed to meet that evening at the Magic Christian, a diner/bar in Yonkers.

The Carrs told the Cassaras about the menacing letter they'd received, and how their dog Harvey had been murdered. They strongly suspected an ex-tenant named Berkowitz.

Cassara's twenty-seven-year-old son Jonah, a hairdresser, also in attendance, then made a crucial deduction. He remembered an odd duck named David Berkowitz who had briefly rented a room in their house in early 1976.

"He never came back for his two-hundred-dollar security deposit after he left," Jonah, between bites of Shrimp Scampi, reminded his dad. "And he was always bothered by Snowball."

Snowball was the Cassara's five-year-old schnauzer, a barking, yapping machine.

Jake Cassara and Sam Carr decided to deliver the letter to the Yonkers Police and convey their suspicions about David Berkowitz. Once again, the police filed the complaint as "Low Priority."

Dear Dad:

I hope you are doing better than I am. You're basking in the sun down there in Miami Beach with your new old wife, I'm colder than a son of a beach in the northeast armpit of the Bronx. That's okay, dad, because the bleak, gloomy weather suits my mood. How would you feel if everyone hated you, if the young and pretty girls mocked and laughed at you even though you never did anything to them?

Why do these pretty girls and their slim boyfriends spit and curse at me, dad? Why do they force me to swerve and step in dog poo? Do you realize how difficult it is to scrape that dog poo off your shoes. It's degrading, dad. But that's all right, things will get better, I know they will.

Clearly the letter to his father was a plea for help. After writing it, David Berkowitz locked himself in his tiny apartment for five-and-a-half weeks, leaving only for Spam, Pepsi and the Daily News, listening to a.m. radio and masturbating. Not making his bed, not flushing the toilet.

Arguably, David's stepfather, Nat, should not have left his son alone, but hindsight is always 20/20, and David was 24-years-old and an army vet. Nat was heart-broken after Pearl, his wife of 33 years, had died of breast cancer. When he met the widow Sylvia at a "mix" sponsored by the Co-op City temple, they discovered their mutual isolation, one thing led to another, and now Nat was remarried to Sylvia and living in a one bedroom condo in Miami Beach. Without David. That was one of the bride's stipulations.

When David finally emerged from his self-imposed isolation it was nearly Xmas, time to kill. That's what old man Sam's voice was telling him. On December 29, 1975, at 8:15 p.m., David took a large serrated butcher knife and drove around the Bronx for hours looking

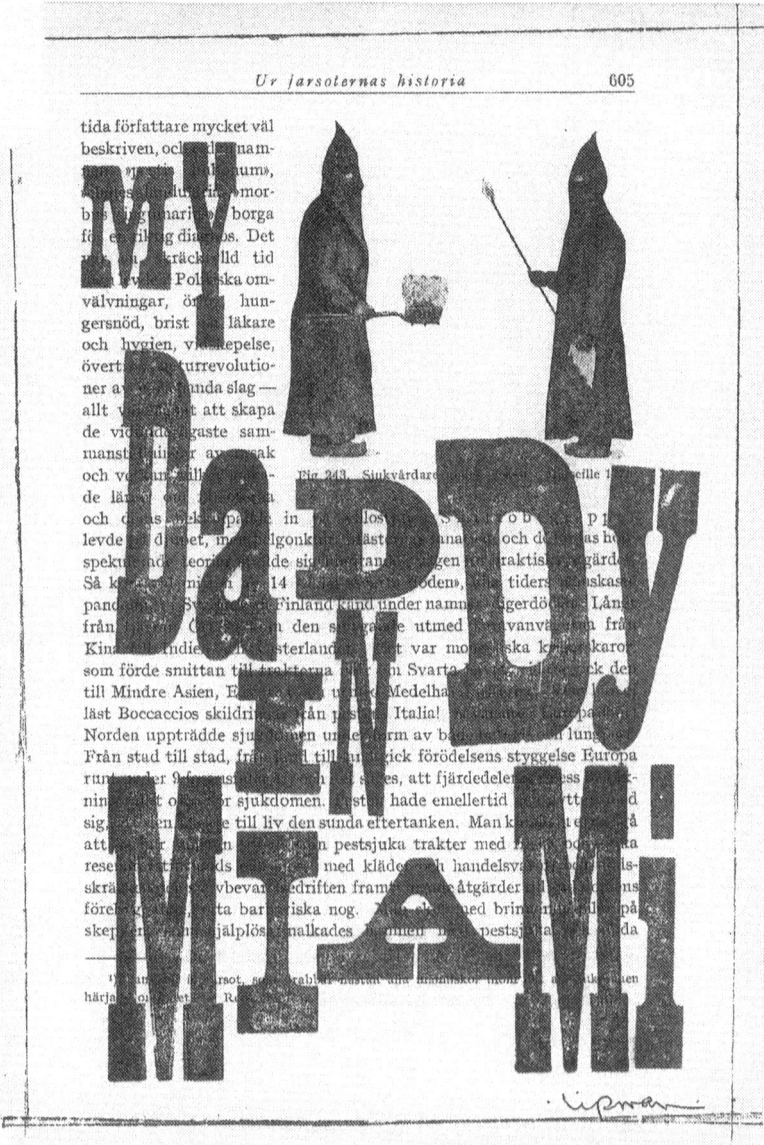

for a young female to "slice and dice." Old Sam would let him know when he found the right one.

As it turned out, David, using the butcher knife, assaulted three females on three different occasions and bungled each one. Old Sam instructed him to switch to a large caliber handgun.

Dear Jimmy Breslin:

Greetings from the gutters of the Big A, and from the vermin that dwell in those gutters and feed on the dried blood that has coagulated in the cracks and crevices of those gutters.

Greetings from the gutters filled with dog poo, vomited sweet wine, piss, and blood. I greet you from the NYC sewers that swallow up these delicacies when they are washed away with sweeper trucks piloted by yahoos.

You fat Irish sack of suds, I feel like I know you. You're a beer drinker, right? A shot of Bushmills, a chase of beer. You sure as hell must be addled when you write about me, Breslin. I'm not a "psychotic fat nobody" like you said. When I turned my back on the boxing game, I was one fight away from being a contender for the welterweight crown. Does that sound like a nobody, you fat hunk of snot? Would you be prepared to strip down and take me on, mano a mano? Can you still see your pecker over your tummy?

Listen carefully, you tub of barf: Because you didn't hear from me for a while doesn't mean I've given up my call. I am still here, a displaced spirit roaming the night, needing to appease Sam.

When I don't find a worthy subject, I return to a scene of an earlier murder and nose around, examining the remnants of blood-stains, police chalkmarks. I've gone to the funerals of some of my girls. And afterwards I've followed the attending cops to the bars or donut shops. Sometimes I've gone to a batting range to take a few swats.

You crave your suds, don't you, Breslin? Well, old Sam craves his blood, and he won't let me stop killing until he gets his fill of the red stuff. Tell me, thick ass, what will you be drinking on the night of July 29, 1977? I know what I'll be drinking. Until then, I say goodbye, and don't forget about Bonnie Capra. She was a very sweet girl.

Thank you for sharing,
SOS

The Daily News, Breslin's newspaper, withheld a portion of the letter at the insistence of the police task force. The omitted portion read: "Here are some names to help your flabby ass get rolling: John Wheaties, Wicked King Wicker, General Jack Cosmo, and The Womb Raider, rapist and suffocator of young gals. Now go fish, Breslin."

The police intelligence unit was intensely researching and decoding those names.

Eighteen-year-old Bonnie Capra was Son of Sam's first victim a year ago, on July 29, 1976, a bubbly brunette gunned down in her canary-yellow Plymouth Duster where she sat alongside her friend, nineteen-year-old Cindi Palantonio, outside Bonnie's Fordham Road apartment (that's in the West Bronx) at 10:50 pm on a Tuesday. Sam used his trademark Charter Arms .44 Bulldog revolver, blasting the two friends at point blank range. Cindi, who was not hit head-on, recovered, though with only some of her wits intact.

With the anniversary of the first murder coming close, the city was in a panic.

By now the police knew they were dealing with a paranoid schizophrenic who considered himself possessed of demonic power, an isolated loner who had difficulty with relationships, especially with women.

Operation Omega, meanwhile, was growing in size and resources, and now contained more than two hundred detectives city wide. It was too big an operation to be in the hands of a captain, so Assistant Police Commissioner Timothy X. Hanifan was given the reins, with Captain Mitch O'Reilly as his deputy.

Dear Hanifan:

I hope you don't mind me referring to you by your surname. You're a big muck-a-muck by cop standards, right? You worked yourself up from foot patrol to one below top dog. And you didn't take any graft along the way; well, you never got caught, anyway. You have a gut, a touch of arthritis, and your hearing ain't what it used to be, but you're not yet in your dotage. If you nail Son of Sam, it could mean finally rising to your highest level of incompetence: Police Commissioner.

Though I'm not an admirer of cops, I feel for you, Hanifan, with your fat gut, defective hearing and sweeping ambition. I will tell you, then, that a SOS strike is imminent. It will happen on the anniversary of the first glorious murder, and will take place in the vested borough of Queens where the girls and wemon are soooo pretty.

I hope this anniversary murder will finally appease old Sam. To look at him, he's a wasted old man, with farty breath, unappealing in the extreme. But what an appetite for blood! It rivals your appetite for power.
So that's where it stands, Hanifan. You be ready on 7/29/77.

41

If you don't find me at the scene of the crime, scour the nearby donut shops and batting ranges. I used to play a little baseball, third base. Struck out a bunch, but I still like to get my swats.

I don't want to murder any more, Hanifan. And without murder there ain't no reason to hang around this fucked-over planet. When your men in their Omega task force camo Swat suits spot me, have them shoot to kill. Blast my ass into the gutter, Commissioner. The raunchier the gutter the better.

Your comrade,
Son of Sam

Hanifan and his top aides closely analyzed the letter. Doctor Myron C. Kessel interpreted SOS's plea to be "blasted" in the gutter as an example of "a self-esteem lack, and very possibly a suicide wish." That the last murder would occur in Queens, Dr. Kessel interpreted as a reference to the mother SOS never had. "His preference would be to elevate, even sanctify, females (Queens), but his degraded condition constrained him to kill them."

Hanifan covered Queens like a cheap suit, with police sharpshooters on roofs and two plainclothes cops in every donut shop in the borough. The batting ranges were also patrolled.

Okay, Son of Sam, you murdering motherfucker. The Big Apple's finest are poised and ready. Let's get it on!

Cool. Only SOS didn't strike on the anniversary date. He struck two days later, not in Queens but in the Gravesend section of Brooklyn. At one-forty a.m., vivacious twenty-year old Heather-Lee Trammell and her vibrant young boyfriend Tony Demarco were spooning in the back of Demarco's dad's silver 1976 Chrysler New Yorker.

Tony had finally managed to undo Heather-Lee's bra strap when they were undone by Berkowitz. Heather-Lee shot once in the head, Tony twice in the face.

Thirty-eight hours later Heather-Lee Trammell was pronounced dead on the operating table. Tony Demarco survived the attack, but without his left eye and a portion of his cheek and nose which had been shot away.

Meanwhile, in Yonkers: Responding to a call from a Craig Glassman about suspected arson at 35 Pine Street, Officers Rickerts and Civiello, recovered three bullets which had been tossed into a fire outside Glassman's door. Evidently the flames didn't get hot enough to set the bullets off.

Glassman, himself a deputy sheriff, interviewed by the police, suspected a tenant from an adjoining building who had been complaining about Glassman's barking golden retriever. The complainant's name was David Berkowitz.

When the rounds were analyzed, it was determined that they came from a Charter Arms .44 Bulldog revolver.

Instead of contacting the city-wide Omega Task Force, the Yonkers cops decided to cop the glory. They staked out Berkowitz's apartment, and at 7:42 p.m. on 8/10/77, a heavyset male wearing a yellow rain slicker, black and white hightop sneakers and carrying a brown paper bag emerged from the apartment and opened the driving side door of a '73 Ford Galaxy. As soon as he settled into the seat, Officer Civiello came from the rear of the car, put the barrel of his Colt .45 against the male's skull and barked: "Freeze. Police."

Civiello's partner Rickerts had come around the other side with his Colt drawn.

The male inside the car turned slowly to Rickerts then to Civiello. He smiled moronically.

"Now that we got you," Civiello said, "Who have we got?"

Still grinning, the male said: "You've just won the lottery, brother cop. *Moi? Je suis* Son of Sam."

David Berkowitz would plead guilty to the Son of Sam murders and be sentenced to 365 years in Attica.

9/5/86

Attica
Dear Pen Pal Dee-Dee,

Greetings from Death Row.

I'd say that that sweaty fat lady that's giving you grief is living on overtime. Why right now her bloodstream may be filling with fatty cholesterol which could cause sudden death or stroke. If you're lucky she will drop dead right at your feet, sliding off the chair and plopping on the floor of the office, and leaving a large greasy stain.

Dee-Dee, I know a lot about fat people. They've eaten themselves to madness and insanity. It's true, Dee-Dee. These gluttons become extremely jealous, self-conscious and finally paranoid, convinced that everyone is laughing at them (which is probably true). They are generally weak-minded, lack will power, self confidence, and are constipated, destructive and even sadistic. Here's what I'd recommend:

Obtain a brown paper lunch bag.
Get a huge hunk of hero bread.
Get plenty of meatballs.
Get plenty of tomato sauce.
Put meatballs and sauce on hero bread.
Secure a fat juicy pickle.
Cut a huge wedge of coconut custard pie.
Put hero wedge, pickle and pie into a brown bag.
At lunchtime get a seat in front of fatso and pull out your hero, pickle, pie lunch.
Ummmmmmm!
Start chewing and watch her drool.
Watch her get dizzy.
Watch her eyes begin to pop out of their sockets.

See fatty run.
See her run out the door.
See her make tracks to Harvey's Hero Haven.
See her bite into a meatball and peppers hero and die.
See fat Sadie dead and buried.
Here lay Fat Sadie whose heart quit at 479 pounds.

Write me again soon, Dee-Dee. I'm thinking of becoming a
born-again.

Love,
Dave

●Wuornos●

Dear Lee Wuornos,

My name is Helga-Lee Uberroth, I'm born-again. I breed horses and wolves and live outside Ocala.

You're going to think I'm crazy, but Jesus told me to write you. I looked into your eyes in one of those newspaper pictures and knew immediately that you were innocent. Then I prayed real hard to Jesus and He confirmed what I felt, in spades.

What I believe with all my heart is that if only the world would know the real Aileen Wuornos, there's not a jury in the entire state of Florida that would convict you.

You and me—we even have the same Christian name. You're Aileen, called Lee. I'm Helga-Lee. I know that is not a coincidence. God bless you, dear child. Please call me collect.

Helga-Lee Uberroth

She breeds horses and wolves and is a born-again Christian? Not your usual configuration.

She also waters her houseplants bare-breasted. She has a green thumb.

With or without breast implants?

Without.

What happens next?

Nine days after receiving the letter, Lee Wuornos phones Helga-Lee collect. Then Helga-Lee visits Lee in the Volusia County Jail. Condemned killers are lonely. The two Lees form a band.

Rock? Rap? Reggae? Zydeco?

Sorry. I meant "bond." They form a bond.

[pause]

Helga-Lee calls Wuornos child. But they're pretty close in age, right?

Helga-Lee is 41, Taurus. Lee is 36, Aries.

Bull and ram. Sounds like fireworks. This the first hard time Wuornos has done?

Noo. She serves 16 months for holding up a convenience store in Pensacola. Plus she spends a bunch of overnights in jails up and down Florida for prostitution. Remember, she's been on her own since adolescence.

She comes from a dysfunctional family, am I right?

You tell me. Her father, Leo Dale Pittman, is a convicted child molester who's beaten by other inmates and finally strangled to death in prison. Her mother, Diane, who marries Pittman when she is fifteen, abandons Lee and her brother Keith after her husband is imprisoned. The children—Lee is seven months old—are adopted by their rigidly

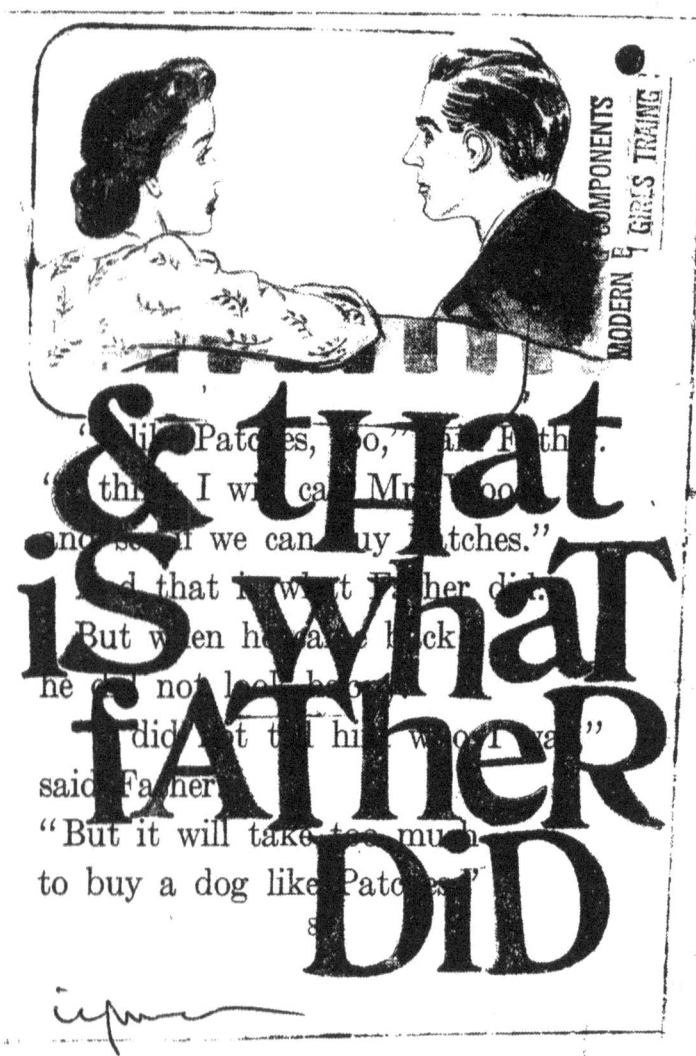

moralistic maternal grandparents, Arnul and Britta Wuornos, and go to live in Troy, Michigan. Lee becomes pregnant at age 12 and is sent to an institution for unwed mothers. After delivering a boy, who is put up for adoption, Lee, 13, is on her own, smokin' weed, slammin' beer, crashing where she can, hitchhiking, balling johns. Meanwhile, her grandmother dies of lung cancer and her grandfather hangs himself from a pepper tree. Her brother Keith either jumps or falls through the sixth story window of an auto parts warehouse in Flint, Michigan. Diane, her mother, remarries for the fourth time and moves to Okinawa, never to be heard from again.

[pause]

When does the rock and roll lawyer get into the picture?

Helga-Lee advises Lee to dump her public defenders, who she claims are incompetent and on the take. She recommends Harvey Medved.

The Jewish Springsteen.

Medved is a sort of unorthodox private defense attorney in practice for half-a-dozen years in central Florida. He looks like a rabbinical student: fat, carrot-red hair, bushy beard. He does hokey singing ads for his law practice on TV. He smokes weed. In a former life he played bass and was lead vocalist for a hard-driving rock band called the Bellevues. Out of Queens, NY.

Where in Queens?

Flushing.

I had a feeling. Is Medved a Jew for Jesus?

No.

Does he water his houseplants bare-breasted with his titties jiggling?

No.

So what do the fat, rabbinical, weed-smoking, hard driving rocker-lawyer and Helga-Lee have in common?

They both end up making money out of Wuornos. Did they arrange a scam from the outset? Hard to say.

[pause]

At what point does Helga-Lee decide to adopt Lee Wuornos?

Soon after Lee testifies in court that she had sex with 250,000 johns.

Whole lotta penises. The court admits that claim?

Florida has something called the Williams Rule, which admits as evidence whatever information might establish a pattern. Technically, Lee Wuornos is being tried for the murder of Richard Mallory, but both her public defenders and the prosecution think they could make good use of the 250,000 johns. The prosecution portrays her as a sex-addict, moronically compulsive; the defense claims that all the abuse she suffers balling and blowing 250,000 johns finally reaches the boiling point.

Neither side questions the figure? 250,000?

Both sides think it's exaggerated, but maybe by not that much. One thing—probably the only thing—Lee has been blessed with is robust health. She was an exit to exit freeway ho who worked fast. She was known for how fast she worked. Plus she's been doing it since age 14.

In the clips I saw Lee Wuornos didn't look all that robust.

Well, her face was shot from all the booze, speed, rough sex, lack of sleep. You couldn't really see her bone structure through the prison garb. But Lee Wuornos is—was—a strapping, big-boned female. Very imposing. The opposite of her namesake and step-mom, the demure Helga-Lee Uberroth.

They're already tight. Why does Helga-Lee want to adopt Wuornos?

Could have to do with getting closer to the big money Lee is likely to make through books and articles and movies. The new law is that inmates cannot profit from their crimes, but if the money is channeled to her adoptive mother…

[pause]

You say that the robust Wuornos works fast. Question is, how does the demure, gentrified, born-again wolf breeder who waters her houseplants bare-breasted win over a tough customer like Wuornos so fast?

"Soul-binding" is how Helga Lee characterizes it in a *People* interview. "We're like Jonathan and David in the Bible," she says. "A chunk of her heart is with me, and a chunk of my heart is with her trapped in jail. We always know just what the other Lee is thinking and feeling. It's uncanny."

*The dollars from Helga-Lee's **People** interview —where does that go?*

Not just *People. Vanity Fair* interviews her. *The New Yorker. The Enquirer. Details.* Wuornos claims never to have received a dime from any of the publicity. Since it's unlawful to profit from your crime, I assume that if the money is not set aside in a trust of some kind, Helga-Lee pockets it.

Lee Wuornos has no living relatives, right? And she herself is about to be fried. So a trust can't be of any use to her.

True.

[pause]

And now we come to that significant other in Lee's life. Drum roll, please, for The Bottom!

That would be Tyria Moore. Bottom doesn't really do her justice. Ty is a motel maid, but she's more than that.

Tell me.

Passion. Tender passion, even. That's the reason Lee remains so loyal to her?

Plus she smells good.

Who?

Tyria Moore. Doesn't Lee say that somewhere?

Probably. Ty is chubby, baby-faced.

She cops a plea.

Betrays Lee is what she does. But you know what? Lee refuses to incriminate her in any of the murders, and she never stops professing her love for Ty.

That's impressive in its way.

Together they live a squalid life. Ty's work is seasonal, meaning she's out of work about as often as not. And Lee ain't a successful ho. Even with her alleged 250,000 johns. Like I said, she's raw-boned and her manner is harsh, even hostile. Not the attributes that will make her good money on the highway. Which in turn contributes to her murderous rage. Lee and Ty rent cheap motel rooms by the week. Sometimes they sleep in their old Chevy pickup, or in deserted barns. They drink a lot of beer. They argue, sure, but there is love there. Lee calls herself Susan Blahovec.

How come?

It's the name of a classmate in junior high school that she had a crush on. Doesn't seem to interfere with her love for Ty.

What kind of love? SM? Blood sports?

No. No way. Maybe now and then watersports. After a night of slammin' beer. Lee drinks Coors Lite to keep the calories down, make her more appealing to the highway johns, but the thing is she drinks a whole lot and the watery brew makes her pee.

[pause]

Lee's accused of killing seven johns?

Right.

Where and when?

Between December '89 and November '90. From central Florida west to the Gulf Coast. Richard Mallory is first, the john she's being tried for. She claims he beat her and raped her. Forcibly sodomized her.

Is that how Wuornos puts it? Forcibly sodomized?

What Wuornos testifies at the trial is: "I told him No, but he— pardon my Greek, I'm a street person—fucked me in the ass which messed up my head. 'Cuz I don't do that shit."

She says that about all seven, doesn't she?

What she testifies is that Mallory violently rapes her. The other six attempt to rape her but she kills them first. In Mallory's instance it could be true. He has a history as a wife-beater and is a registered violent sex offender.

Registered where?

In the sovereign state of Florida.

[pause]

What's he—Mallory—do when he's not forcibly sodomizing hoes?

Used car dealer in Lake City. GMC and Ford. He won't sell, or even drive, a foreign car.

The six others?

Dick Monday, Troy Burress, Duane Spears, Chuck Carskaddon,

Walter Gino Puglia, Pete Siems. Working-class stiffs looking for a quick hump. Or maybe a blowjob between exits on the highway. Are they all into sadistically beating Lee up? Well, the jury doesn't buy it. Each is shot several times in the front and back with the same Smith and Wesson .38 Police Special.

Has Helga-Lee ever blown a john in his American-made pickup while he's gunning it up or down the highway?

Helga-Lee is widowed and childless. I guess I didn't say that. Her husband was thirty-something years older and had money. She's into horses and wolves, not johns. She's never, ever used her mouth in a salacious manner.

[pause]

So when do Lee, Helga-Lee and the Jewish Springsteen finally converge?

Soon after Lee ditches her court-appointed defenders. They converge in the Volusia County Jail where Lee is being held. That's in Daytona, by the way.

Lee is impressed?

With Medved? Evidently. He's fat but he's smooth. He's Jewish so he doesn't have that macho thing Lee hates.

Medved takes over. Then what?

Lee intends to plead innocent by virtue of self-defense. The facts of Richard Mallory's wife-beating past appear to corroborate her claims of violent rape. But Medved convinces her to plead guilty.

Why?

He assures Lee that pleading innocent would fail but that a guilty plea, with the mitigating evidence of Mallory's attempted rape, would likely get her a reduced sentence, which, with good behavior, could mean she's out in five years.

She bites?

Reluctantly. Pressured by both Medved and her adoptive mother, Helga-Lee.

What's their real motive?

I'm just speculating. Get Lee executed so they can continue to make money from the movies, TV specials, books and such, without Lee's angry protestations?

Which is what happens, right?

Pretty much. In the process Lee turns violently against them, identifies them as her enemies along with the 250,000 would-be rapist johns. Along with most of American culture.

Lee Wuornos has it in for a whole lot of folks, right?

Ha. Once, when Helga-Lee and Medved accompany a British film director who wants to shoot a documentary on Lee to the Volusia County Jail, Lee physically attacks Helga-Lee and has to be restrained. It takes three guards to actually strait-jacket her as she is screaming at Helga-Lee and Medved. She calls Helga-Lee "a money-crazy pimp for Jesus" and Medved "a tub of snot." The film-maker records it all. The documentary, called *Women Do it Better*, wins a bunch of awards, including something at Sundance. The story is that Helga-Lee and Medved get a fat cut.

Evil. What finally happens at the trial?

The jury deliberates for less than an hour, then finds Lee guilty of first-degree murder. They recommend that Judge Uriel Blount sentence her to death in Old Sparky, the infamously malfunctioning electric chair. Which is what he does. As Lee is led out of the courtroom, she pulls away from the bailiff and screams at the jurors: "I'm innocent! I was raped. Scumbags of America, I hope you all get raped in the ass!"

You know what. If they all get raped in the ass they'll still be scumbags.

You could be right.

[pause]

Now that Wuornos is history, consigned to the Discovery channel, are the weed-smoking, bushy-bearded rabbinical lawyer and the born-again wolf-breeder who waters her houseplants bare-breasted still an item?

To be honest, my interest in the case flags after Wuornos is executed. What the odd couple has been up to post-Lee Wuornos, I can't tell you.

☻Big Ed☻

One part of me wanted to ask her for a date.

The other part kept wondering how her head would look on a stick.

Welcome to the *Künstforum*, my name is Edmund Kemper the Third.

Künst in Deutsch means art, which is what I am, an artist.

I also like the sound of it: *Künst.*

What kind of art? I murder folks.

I thumped about a dozen, a baker's dozen, including my paternal grandparents and my mom.

Clarnell is—was—her name.

Odd name for a standard brand bitch.

I could never get her to shut her hole.

After I cut off her head, I cut out her larynx—vocal cords to you voyeuristic yahoos out there in Google land.

When I dumped her cords in the trash compactor it spit them back out, almost caught me in the eye.

Without a head and with her larynx cut out I still couldn't shut her up.

So I fucked her, and, guess what?, she didn't make a sound.

Well, there were some animal noises, gasses and such, and the smells that went along with them, but that's cool, I like raunchy smells.

I like the smells of dead things.

I said I was Edmund Kemper the Third.

My dad was E.E. Kemper the Second, he died of colon cancer before I could murder him.

Too much poop in his large intestine, got all wound around and festered.

Smelled godawful.

E.E. Kemper the Second.

Actually he was okay, as humans go, he was big like me, though not as big.

He was also smart like me, though not as smart.

Me, I'm the biggest and smartest serial killer that ever fucking was.

Six-feet-nine-and-a-half, 312 pounds stark raving neggid.

My IQ is conservatively estimated at 148, conservative because when I was tested here at Folsom sixteen months ago the tester was a loutish guard drunk on cheap gin.

And I had just recovered from a suicide attempt.

Stabbed myself in the jugular with a ball point pen.

Not to worry, I was just making theater.

There ain't a ball point pen in the civilized world big enough to snuff Big Ed Kemper the Third.

The prison bones took it seriously, sent me to the psych ward, which is a whole other animal.

I'll detail that for you in the next installment.

I said I thumped a baker's dozen, right?

They only nailed me for ten.

Murders, like mothers, are not always for public consumption.

A murder done just right is an autistic—I mean artistic—act.

It is an intimate, even sacred, act.

All that blood, all dem passions.

What comes after the murder also counts.

The beheading, the dissection, the dining in, the good old-fashioned necro-fuck.

I've heard folks say: What's the point of fucking a corpse! You end up doing all the work.

Not so, trust me.

A properly beheaded, dissected, cannibalized coed—or mom, for that matter—can be a delectable bedmate.

But only if you're sensitive and attend to the small things:

emissions, chemical smells, gasses, the occasional—but always welcome—spasm.

Any self-respecting female partner alive will contain her gasses and emissions, and that's unfortunate if the male partner prefers to go the whole nine.

Whereas when she's dead the morals relax, the fluids dispense, the smells are multiple and varied and definitely on the raunchy side.

For me that's a plus.

Those two or three killings I didn't 'fess up to I carry with me in an intimate place.

A downy skin-pouch next to my testes.

The skin-pouch is human, *naturellement*.

My testes, you wonder?

Capacious, voluminous, incomprehensible, Brobdingnagian.

I said I was 6-9-and-a-half, okay?

Big Ed wears big suspenders.

I was 6-8 when I was fifteen which is when I snuffed grandma Jolie and grandpa Edmund the First.

I was staying with them at their ranch outside Crescent City, CA, near the Oregon border, where my mom in her wisdom had exiled me.

Jolie and Ed were scared shitless of their massive, moody grandson, 6-8, 285, wearing glasses, not flushing the toilet, shambling around the house with his boots unlaced, shooting gophers and skunks and birds with his Remington .22.

Grandma Jolie said: Eddie, don't shoot the birds, but I'd shoot them anyway and, when I felt like it, bring the carcasses back and toss them on the kitchen table.

Crows, blackbirds, a few mockingbirds that were keeping me awake at night, assorted sparrows, three or four squawking Stellers jays with their funny crests, robins of course, a large hawk with a banded tail, various rat-a-tat-tat woodpeckers.

Well, I tossed two dead jays and a beheaded skunk on to the big wooden kitchen table while Grandma Jolie was sitting there peeling potatotes.

It was two-fifteen pm on a Tuesday.

The dead animals made a loud splat and slithered bloodily across the table.

Grandma Jolie was just about to raise a fuss when I pointed my Remington at her and shot her in the face.

She fell back against the chair, then forward into the bowl of partially peeled potatoes.

I pulled her dead head up by the hair and settled it flush into the bowl of potatoes.

It looked funny that way.

I heard my granddad, Edmund Kemper the First, returning from the grocery store in Crescent City.

I reloaded fast and hopped outside.

I bagged him as he was getting out of the GMC longbed pickup.

Got him in the chest.

Then sauntered up to him and zapped him in the head, just like we were doing to the gooks over there in 'Nam.

This was in '65.

After I ate I got into his truck and drove to the police station in Crescent City.

What did I eat? I ate my granddad.

Just kidding.

I ate some of the groceries: sweet rolls and Spam. Drank four Dr. Peppers. I was thirsty.

I said I was fifteen, too young to do hard time.

So they labeled me schizophrenic and stuck me in Perdido State Hospital for the Criminally Insane up there in Humboldt County.

Don't jump the gun: it wasn't as bad a gig as it sounds.

Accessing another part of my personality, I became a team player.

What I really did was learn the moronic syntax of Perdido State Hospital and play the role.

Meanwhile I sat at the feet of mass and serial murderers.

Eccentric, most of them, but masters of their craft.

They let me out in 68.

I had grown to my full size: 6-9-and-a-half, between 310 and 330 pounds.

A gargantuan anti-hippie who went back to live with his mom.

Hippies were unwashed Godless slackers.

Clarnell, divorced from her second husband, I think his name was Hank, had gotten a secretarial job at UC Santa Cruz, and I manipulated a campus sticker, which meant I could park on campus.

Which meant hitchhiking coeds would see the sticker and assume I was kosher.

It would be the last assumption they'd make.

Anita and Ella Jo were studying literature and art history, or maybe it was marketing and home economics.

Coeds, blond all over, hippy cute, hitching on Highway 1 north.

When I stopped the car they looked at me doubtfully.

I smiled and pointed to the sticker on the back window, driver's side.

When they saw that they looked at each other then slid into the kelly green Plymouth Duster.

We'd only traveled about three miles when I picked up the .22 Remington from under the driver's seat, it was already cocked.

Ella Jo, next to me, was having her period, I could smell it, it was getting me roused.

I shot her in the head with the .22.

Then I turned to Anita in the back seat and shot her in the head.

She was wiggling so I shot her again.

I continued driving to the condo where I lived with Clarnell.

Nobody was in the parking lot.

I transferred Anita to the trunk.

I wrapped Ella Jo in a blanket and carried her upstairs.

I took her into the bathroom where I beheaded then dissected her.

Then I brought her into my bedroom and fucked what remained intact, the first time I ever fucked a beheaded, dissected girl on her period.

On occasion I would dine in.

That is, if I was hungry or gamy, so to speak, I would eat a portion of one after I fucked her.

A side of buttock, say, with pink sweet nipple garnish, stir fried with some brown rice.

Once in a while I'd eat before sex.

Which was the more savory sexing, before or after "dining in"?

I'd just as soon keep you guessing on that one.

Truthfully, I varied the sequence in other ways.

The only constant was the beheading.

I can't say why I was so stuck on beheading.

It had been a fantasy since I was a child.

And it facilitated my intention that the corpse, if discovered, be hard to identify.

Ella Jo was small, I flushed chunks of her down the toilet, which had an unusually powerful flushing action.

Then I drove to the ocean and flung two compact-sized trash bags of Ella Jo into the sea, beyond the surf, fish-food.

I have always had a strong arm, and at 6-9-and-a-half, I have a certain leverage.

I retained Ella Jo's pert blond head, which I put into the trunk next to her friend Anita.

Then I drove to Berkeley for an appointment with my court-appointed psychiatrist.

His name was Levinson.

He gazed at me a long time over his glasses.

He asked some questions.

He said that I seemed to be making progress.

When I got back to the condo I beheaded, ate, dissected and fucked Anita.

I disposed of her hands and head in Oakland and the rest of her in the fair city of Orinda.

For the next few weeks I didn't do much.

Played one-man chess, read texts on anatomy and dissection,

masturbated.

The police managed to discover some of little Ella Jo's remains and to deduce that they belonged to Ella Jo.

Re the murderer, they admitted to being stumped.

On the domestic front, Clarnell and I weren't getting along.

We were in each other's face just about every day.

But on Tuesday, 5, February 1973, we had a particularly nasty row.

I stormed out of the condo and slammed the door.

It was twenty to eight in the pm.

I drove toward the UCSC campus when I saw Ruby hitching a ride in the other direction.

She had long wavy black hair.

I swung a U and picked her up.

A few miles farther I saw tall, slender Debbie hitching and stopped the Duster.

When she saw Ruby in the front seat next to me and the UC parking sticker on the windshield she hopped into the back.

I drove for another four or five miles.

The highway as usual was sparsely traveled.

Because of the crap with Clarnell, I was feeling reckless.

I took out a machete from under the driver's seat and in one motion sliced Ruby's throat.

The arterial blood squirted everywhere.

I heard Debbie gasp in the back seat.

I turned and waved the bloody machete at her and told her to keep quiet or I would kill her right there.

She started to weep and sob.

I took a sharp left off the freeway onto a maintenance road, stopped the Duster, pulled bleeding Ruby out.

Debbie was still sobbing, I opened the door, dragged her out by the hair, then, using my left hand and right forearm, snapped her neck with one quick motion.

I'd always wanted to try that and it worked just like it was drawn up.

The maintenance road was deserted, so I beheaded the two girls and fitted them into the trunk.

I kept Debbie's head under the driver's seat.

The Duster was so bloody a little more blood wouldn't matter.

Then on impulse, I removed Ruby from the trunk, laid her out on the asphalt, stuck Debbie's head on Ruby's shoulders, and fucked the dead composite right there.

Would that officially qualify as a *menage-a-trois*? I hope so.

I fitted them—heads and carcasses—in the trunk and drove to Clarnell's condo.

I didn't think a small girl could bleed so much, both front seats were drenched with blood.

Kind of a heavy sweet smell with some acrid around the edges.

The killing and fucking were good and I liked bloody Ruby's smell, but I wasn't finished.

I was still feeling pent-up because of Clarnell.

My mom's car wasn't in its spot, so I carried the headless Debbie upstairs and dissected her in the bathtub.

I'm a very big man and I hadn't eaten for several hours, so I fried some buttock in olive oil, sliced a seeded baguette, added mayo, and had a tender-assed hero sandwich.

Scratch that: a hero has to be made with Italian bread.

What I ate professed to be French.

Did I say that Santa Cruz was the"Harvard of the West?"

When I tried to flush small chunks of Debbie in the toilet the toilet backed up and flooded onto the floor.

I turned off the water and looked for the plumber's helper, but couldn't find it.

Just then, I heard the key turn in the lock: Clarnell.

She'd seen my Duster in the lot, so she knew I was back.

Immediately she started screaming.

"What's that smell? And what's this—blood? What are you doing in there?'

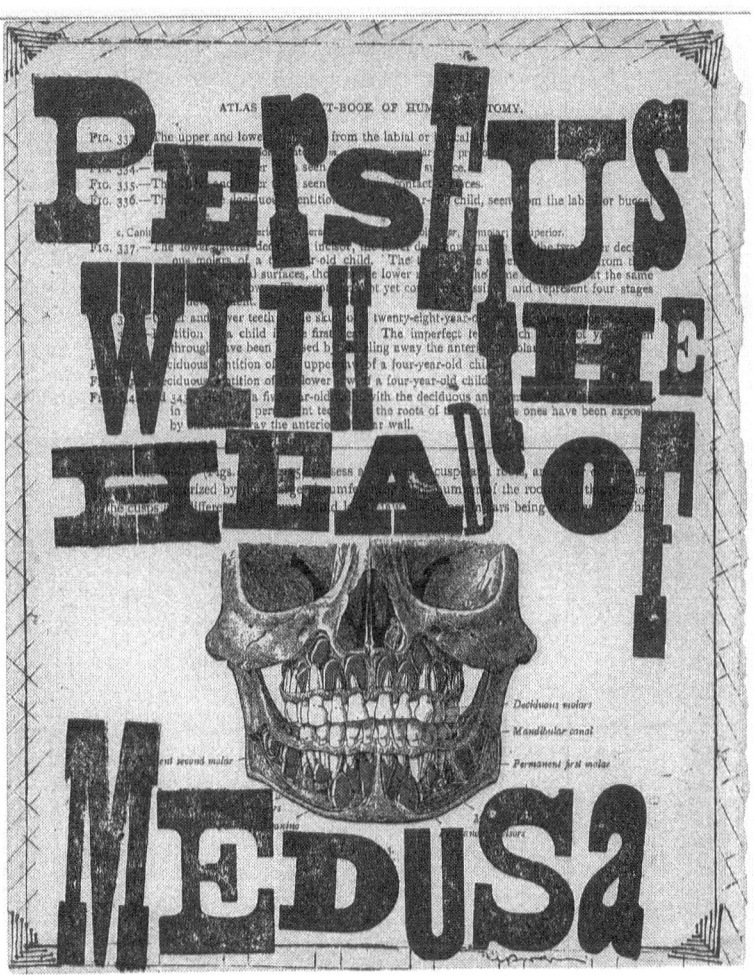

I didn't respond.

"I said what are you doing in there?"

Still no response from Big Ed.

"You animal. I'm dialing 911."

At that, I flung open the bathroom door and stormed out like Norman Bates waving the bloody machete.

Her mouth was open, ready to scream, but I got to her before she could get it out.

Swung smartly at her neck and caught enough of it to kill her, she fell heavily onto her left side.

I lifted her by her dyed, stiff blond hair and sliced her head off.

Perseus with the head of Medusa.

I excised her larynx like I told you.

Stuffed it into the trash compactor but it spit right back out.

I had to laugh.

I dragged her into her bedroom and fucked her on the bed, but it wasn't like I was fucking Clarnell, my very mean mom.

With her head off she was like any other corpse, just more wrinkled, but I enjoyed fucking her just the same.

Afterwards I stored her in her wardrobe closet.

I thought for a minute what to do next then dialed the number of Clarnell's close friend Sara.

"Close friend" is a euphemism; I was pretty sure they were lesbian lovers.

I was irked when she didn't answer the phone.

It was ten-forty.

I cleaned up the bathroom as best I could and stuck Debbie in the closet with Clarnell.

Then I lay down in Clarnell's bloody bed and fell right asleep.

Interestingly, it was one of the calmest sleeps I'd had in a long time.

The phone woke me up at 8:45. Coincidentally, it was Sara.

I told her that I wanted to have a surprise brunch for Clarnell whose birthday happened to be in three days, 8, February.

Sara hesitated but then agreed to come over.

I whacked her as soon as she came through the door, throttled her with Clarnell's black garter belt which I'd fished out of her drawer.

She passed into Hades with a terror-stricken look on her face.

I beheaded her right where she lay then dragged her into Clarnell's bedroom and fucked her.

Correction: I tried to fuck her but couldn't, don't know why.

It was the first time I'd ever been impotent with a corpse.

I stuck Sara in the closet with her lover Clarnell and slender Debbie.

Three headless gringas.

Between Sara and Clarnell, I collected almost two hundred dollars.

Downstairs I took Sara's beige and maroon Thunderbird and drove south.

I guess I was thinking of Mexico.

Isn't that what Robert Mitchum did in some film noir?

Hell, every fleeing felon in California or Texas aims for Mexico.

Outside Santa Barbara I dumped the Thunderbird and rented a Lincoln with tinted windows, more space for my legs.

On impulse I picked up an Oriental girl, she said she was Korean.

She was waiting for the bus to take her to dancing class, but the bus was slow in coming.

She wouldn't tell me her name.

She seemed somehow to sense what I had in mind, so I responded fast.

With my left hand on the wheel I spanned her thin neck with my large right hand and throttled her.

There were cars on the freeway but the tinted windows gave me some privacy.

I dropped her on the seat, lifeless, devoid of life.

But then she started to moan.

I pulled off the freeway into a stretch of woods, took out my knife and beheaded her.

Then I fucked her.

A dead vagina is more elastic than a live one, but it was still a very tight fit.

The Sara failure was an aberration, I was as potent as ever.

Instead of putting the Oriental girl in the trunk, I just tossed her, body and head, into the woods.

An odd thing happened when I got to Chula Vista, just a few miles north of the Baja, Mexico border.

I found a phone booth and phoned the Santa Cruz police.

I'd killed Clarnell, my very mean mom, and I guess I needed a break.

Maybe I wanted to be punished so that I could repent.

For a while the Santa Cruz police didn't believe me, but then I said some things and they believed me.

I rented a motel room for the night there in Chula Vista.

Room # 23.

I read a few pages of *The Great Gatsby* then turned off the light.

I'd always had a thing for Scott Fitzgerald and wacky Zelda.

I was in a deep dreamless sleep when the cops with guns drawn burst into the room before dawn.

⊕ Dr. K⊖

Sourbraten Hank.

What fellow students called him at Harvard. Because of his foul disposition and thick German accent.

How German was he?

You mean *is*. He's still alive after half-a-dozen hellish bypasses. Fatty deposits in the blood. He's pushing eighty.

Born Alfred Heinz Kissinger, in Fürth, near Nuremberg. Jews were forbidden to live in Nuremberg.

How German is he? As German as his two idealized princes: Metternich and Bismarck, each, in K's eyes, an iron-willed man of action.

Man of action is what Kissinger wasn't.

Not in the usual sense. His brain engaged his passions.

Nuclear family.

Orthodox Jews.

Father was a schoolmaster disenfranchised by the Nazis. By all accounts a passive, frightened man. His mother was the force. She engineered their successful flight to the US in 1938.

1938. Kristallnacht.

Night of the broken glass. Actually several nights in succession. Nazi thugs breaking windows of Jewish businesses, assaulting, murdering Jews throughout the Reich.

Kristallnacht was in November '38, the very month and year the Kissingers fled to the Land of the Free two goosesteps ahead of the Gestapo.

Yet K has consistently denied that his upbringing in Nazi Germany had any effect on his character.

Why deny it?

Probably to elevate his actions as National Security Advisor and Secretary of State.

How much better to derive from the Princes Metternich and Bismark and the transcendental lineage of so-called great statesmen than from his persecuted petit-bourgeois orthodox Jewish family.

Jewish self-hatred?

How did you know?

Educated guess. There was a sibling, wasn't there? A brother?

A younger brother. Walter. Much more extroverted.

People who knew both expressed surprise that it was Henry who became famous. He'd always seemed so out of sorts. Depressed.

At least he wasn't a shirker; he served in the US Army.

Which goes to prove that not all Jews are shirkers.

K enlisted as a private in 1943, was attached to an Intelligence unit and sent to Germany. He rose to the rank of sergeant, but due to unusual circumstances and his knowledge of German, he ended up actually ordering senior American officers.

He relished the power.

When he was demobbed he returned to his parents' apartment in the Washington Heights section of Manhattan.

Soon after he won a NY State scholarship to Harvard.

He excelled in Harvard.

Statistically, yes. But he made no friends.

Correction: he did find a species of friend, a philosophy professor who'd been a war hero. Well-bred WASP. His surname was Elliott. K seemed to idealize him.

Unfailingly cruel to subordinates, K was a ready sycophant. So long as the object of admiration conformed to his heroic ideal of the well-bred man of action.

Kissinger himself is ill-bred, coarse-mannered.

I wouldn't say ill-bred.

Coarse-mannered? Yes, undeniably.

Partly it's his sense of superiority. As he sees it, a great man shouldn't have to put on airs, feign graciousness. Partly it's the way he is constructed. He's always been short, plump, ungainly, though oddly nimble, come to think of it. I associate his nimbleness with the trickster in him.

Trickster or shyster?

Good point. Let's call him a tricky shyster.

He was the playboy of the western world during the Nixon watch.

That was an ongoing visual joke. K escorting starlets and society women who all seemed a head taller than he.

He never bedded any of them.

He once said: "The relationship between a woman and man of my type is unavoidably very complex."

What did he mean by "my type"?

German Jewish.

Ruthlessly ambitious.

Intellectually superior.

Disadvantaged sexually.

One or more of the above, very likely.

Power was his aphrodisiac.
It never gave him a hard-on.
Bombing Cambodia back to the stone age. Assassinating Allende. Revving up the war in Vietnam. Genociding East Timor. Encouraging Pakistan's assault on Bangladesh. Contributing immeasurably to the coup in Cyprus. It all made K feel very sexy.
It never gave him a hard-on.

Sex in the head.
You've seen his *Kopf.* He wears a size eight-and-a-half hat, which is almost unheard of. Outside D.C.

There's some big hat sizes in that town.
You said it.

Peace with honor.
Kissinger's phrase at the signing of the Vietnam peace treaty in Paris in 1973. K himself had torpedoed the treaty South Vietnam was prepared to sign in 1968.
Though associated with the Democratic negotiating team headed by Averell Harriman in '68, K did not want the Johnson-Humphrey Democrats to take credit for ending the abysmal war. So he secretly promised the South Vietnamese better terms under the incoming Republican administration.

Broken promises.
Five years later, in Paris, with Watergate-embattled Nixon in office, the terms for a "peace with honor" turned out to be substantially the same as in 1968.
How many millions of casualties would have been spared in those five years? How much of the land and infrastructure in Vietnam and

Cambodia would have been spared in those five years?

People who like people.

Ah, Streisand.

K never dated her. He preferred non-Jewish famous females.

Liking people? He admitted that as a boy when he saw a group of boys approach he would cross the street.

Ugly people (presumably excluding himself) made him want to throw up.

He did not make a single friend while going to George Washington High School in New York City.

His early ambition was to be an accountant. Numbers over humans.

Would you want him to prepare your taxes?

No. He would overcharge. Along with his unpleasant bedside manner.

Did I say that he secretly bugged his staff?

Bugged their phones?

Phones and correspondence. No specific reason. Testing their loyalty.

Did any fail the test?

Can't say. In K's mind, very likely. When his staff found out they were bugged, they were furious, but that didn't faze Dr. K. He was—is—unconscionable. And his furious staff wasn't ballsy enough to trouble him in any tangible way.

Public Urinals.

Like Andy Warhol, his exact contemporary, K had a phobia about urinating in the company of other males. Well, phobia might be too strong. But he avoided using them.

Wealthy and powerful as he's become, he doesn't have to urinate in public anymore.

When, while dining in a top flight restaurant, he has to pee, the secret service guys make sure the Gentlemen's is void of other males. If there's a problem in the Gents', they'll clear out the Ladies'.

Problem in the Gents'?
Somebody taking a dump in a stall. For K, even that's too close for comfort.

Warhol adored Kissinger.
Unreservedly.

It wasn't reciprocated.
No. K had no aptitude for art. Let alone the slippery stuff Warhol was up to. K is humorless of course so Warhol's deadpan left him cold. And Warhol's queerness had to have made K nervous.

Marcel Duchamp and Kissinger.
Funny story. In Zurich in 1968, shortly before Duchamp's death, Kissinger's hosts took K and his party to a major Duchamp exhibition. Duchamp's famous "ready-made" urinal was among the objects on display.
At the reception afterwards, K took it upon himself to lecture the great Dadaist about what he called the unseemliness of the urinal as a subject for art.
Duchamp, so the story goes, listened silently with a wry expression on his face while smoking his cheroot.

Wasn't Zurich the birthplace of Dada? Cabaret Voltaire?
That datum would have been lost on Dr. K.
I said K was humorless. That's not precisely true. He was known to crack a mordant joke at the expense of a contemporary like Castro or Thatcher or Gerald Ford. He also would occasionally joke about himself, but his self-deprecation was always subtly self-righteous.

Kissinger's first marriage.

First and only. Ann Fleischer. They married in New York City and she accompanied him to Cambridge. Like him, she was a refugee from Germany. But not a student or an intellectual.

The evidence suggests that he treated her shabbily. When he came home in the evening he forbade her from talking to him so as not to disturb his train of thought.

She was quoted as saying that K "withdrew his libido" from her.

Meaning that he stopped fucking her.

Exactly.

Penile pump.

That would be Nelson A. Rockefeller. Another of Kissinger's mentors. Wealthier than Croesus of course, and both a statesman and man of action, in K's view.

K advised Rockefeller in his bids for the presidency in '64 and '68.

And it was K who advised Rockefeller to surgically install—if that's the right word—a penile pump, which ended up killing Rockefeller in a failed attempt to penetrate his secretary, a young woman with glasses, out of Radcliffe.

Though pushing seventy, Rocky was still horny. Or wanted to be. But his heart couldn't handle it.

The "A" in Nelson A. Rockefeller.

Attica.

What does Kissinger know about penile pumps?

The story is that he was getting a kickback—"rakeoff," he called it—from Ely Lilly, the pharmaceutical giant that patented the pump.

Richard Milhous Nixon.

The signal question there is who was ripping off whom? Behind

Nixon's back and in his memoirs K criticized Nixon as being isolated, unforgiving, paranoid, utterly without charm.

Nixon said and wrote approximately the same things about K, with a few dollops of anti-Semitism.

Iago and Iago.

Somehow they pulled it off.

Pulled off what?

Their stand-up comedy routine. Worldwide genocide.

Nixon never used Kissinger's penile pump.

Noo. He had other things to worry about.

But Haldeman and Ehrlichmann both tried it. Liddy too.

G. Gordon Liddy used a penile pump? Liddy with the shaved head and dyed-black mustache. The hardest ass in the Nixon clan. Who used to burn his hand with a cigarette lighter to strengthen his will. Who went to jail without copping a plea—and enjoyed it. You sure about that?

Yes. And the pump didn't work. Deflated him at the indigo moment, so to speak.

Don't invite Liddy and K to the same rave.

Liddy has never forgiven him.

Henry Kissinger post-Millennium.

Making money hand over fist. Peddling his influence to large corporations. Delivering lectures at 125,000 dollars a clip. He's CEO of some animal called Kissinger Associates.

125,000 K a lecture. What does he talk about?

Himself. His accomplishments. His appraisal of political figures. He likes Helmut Kohl. He dislikes Margaret Thatcher. Loathes Fidel Castro. Loathes Idi Amin. That sort of thing.

Henry Kissinger's legacy.

Official First World history has it that he is brilliant, resourceful, prophetic even. Our Nobel Peace Laureate. The statesman of statesmen.

Unofficially.

A serial mass murderer of Hitlerian proportions.

☙ Dr. Death ❧

And now, please put your virtual hands together for Dr. Death.

[Applause]

Dr. Death, welcome. Sit right down there next to Charo.

[Charo makes to hug the doctor, who pulls back violently]

I don't like anyone's hands on me.

She's not anyone Doc; she's Charo. The original coochie-coochie girl. She sang and jiggled with Cugat. She had extensive reconstructive surgery. She's your bona fide TV and Internet talk-show bimbo.

Never mind.

[The doctor sits on the absinthe green leather sofa and crosses his thin legs]

They call you Dr. Death but your real name is Jack Kevorkian?

Correct.

No one has ever called you Jack the Ripper, I suppose.

[Whistles, laughter]

Just yourself.

I see that you're dressed as you always dress: old ratty cardigan, Salvation Army trousers, black, scuffed workshoes. The makeshift clothes and that stark grey crewcut are sort of your signature, right, Doc?

[Kevorkian does not respond]

How many folks have you euthanized?

Euthanized is inaccurate. I have provided assistance for suicides. You want the number? One hundred thirty-two.

[Applause, loud whistling]

Whoa! If you were a serial killer you'd hold the world record.

The world these very sick people inhabited had already killed them. Their hearts beat but they were, for all practical purposes, dead.

[The host is glancing through the publicity material]

And you're not just a medical doctor. You taught yourself how to play the…harpsichord, you are a gifted painter, you speak a bunch of languages—

Just hobbies. I am a pathologist.

[Scattered applause]

About your paintings, they were described as "strikingly well-executed, stark, surreal, and demented or hilarious, depending on your point of view." Is that an accurate description?

Couldn't say. I painted some canvases to raise money for my cause.

Where are they now?

The originals were stolen. I don't want to discuss it. I no longer paint.

Well, you're obviously skilled with your hands. You constructed your own death machine, right?

I didn't have much choice, did I?

How did you build it?

You mean where did I find the materials? The hardware store, garage sales, flea markets. I used an old lawn mower motor.

Sort of like Dr. Frankenstein, right?

Not right. Frankenstein is fiction. I'm talking about harsh reality.

[Loud boos, then laughter, scattered applause]

You even named it—this death machine. What's it called, Doc?

Thanatron.

That's Latin—

Greek. It means death machine.

•poem•

by

sin

glé

drop

290 ...THE NOMINAL... ...EXPERIMENT...

round ...to that th...stopp...ed e...pp...ost. ...he sm...space betw...the stopcock and the end is next two-thirds...d with a stong solution of ammonia and a single drop of the ammonia-solution is suffered to fall...to the chlorine tube, the stopcock being opened for a mome...for...is...pose (Fig. 126). The entrance of this drop into...e atm...pher...f chlorine is marked by a small, lambent, yell...sh-g...n flas...at the point where the drop enters the gas...rop...y drop...t intervals of a few seconds, the ammonia solution is...ed to fall into the

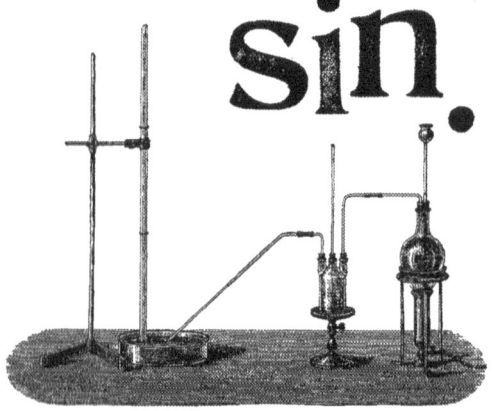

FIG. 1...

chlorine-tu...the...mmon...of...ch...p being converted, at the instant of its...ntact wi...th...chlorine, into hydrochloric acid and nitrogen...flash...lig...the formation of a dense white clou...The...ition...f ammonia must be continued till the whole of the chlorine present is supplied with hydrogen at the expense of ammo...To insure the ammoniacal solution being added in...of th...fo...res is abundantly suf...ent...he result i...hat...droch...ric acid formed com...es w...excess...f am...to fo...a compound, which...res...arance...wh...it...ing

Makes sense. It says here that you've been fascinated with death since you were a kid, performing amateur autopsies on anything dead you could lay your hands on—

Is that what it says?

Right here. I guess you didn't write it yourself, eh?

Nope.

Though you were fascinated with dissection and death, one of your boyhood friends, Rick Dakesian, a fellow Armenian, says that your first love was baseball. That true?

Well, that's what it says on the printout.

Rick Dakesian says that not only could you recite any major league player's batting average, but you knew the pitchers' earned run averages. You even knew their heights and weights and when they were born. Rick said that you actually wanted to be a baseball announcer but that your parents disapproved. That's amazing.

Why?

Because baseball is fun, and fun ain't exactly the first thing that comes to mind when the name Dr. Death is mentioned. You still follow baseball?

No. Between my work and answering moronic questions from Internet hosts, I have no time for games.

[Boos, scattered hisses, laughter]

Your work is of course death in many of its guises, and it is clear that you've attained a comfort level in what you're doing. You're familiar with the bumper sticker: "Death Sucks," right?

What's the question?

The big D. Death. You don't seem to be scared shitless of it like the rest of us earthlings.

Billions have died on this depleted planet of ours, okay? The dead must wonder, in their vegetable way, what the fuss is about. After all, how excruciating can nothingness be?

[pause]

You're asking me, Doc?

You have something to add?

[Charo chimes in]

Death. I no frightened of *eet*.

[Doctor Death addresses Charo from the opposite end of the long leather sofa]

So you expect to end up in heaven?

Me? Jes. I go up there.

[The host]

What about you, Doctor Death? Will you end up in heaven? Or

will those 132 assisted suicides stand in your way?

What stands in my way are pious fools and cowardly bureaucrats.

You've murdered—that is, assisted—132 would-be suicides and not been prosecuted. What else do you want?

I want to transfuse blood from a freshly dead cadaver to a human in need. With his permission, I want to put the condemned criminal in a deep, drugged sleep, conduct experiments on his body; then, when the experiments are completed, I want to execute the prisoner humanely, by injection.

[Catcalls, loud yodeling]

I want to videotape the eyes of a person passing from life to death. I want to remove the stomach, pancreas, and kidneys from a full term infant born with severe spina bifida, paraplegia, and hydrocephalus.

Why? Why do you want to do those things?

Think for a minute. Because you're an Internet host in a shiny suit with surgically repaired features and a hair weave shouldn't prevent you from thinking.

Thanks a lot, Doc. Okay, you're removing organs from live people—

Condemned people. Hopeless cases. The irreparably doomed.

Got it. You're experimenting on hopeless cases for the sake of science.

Correct. That great abstraction Science.

[Mocking hoots and whistles, scattered applause]

You've made more than your share of enemies among fellow scientists. Is that a fair statement, Dr. Death?

You say "scientists" as if it's a privileged category. Scientists, like lawyers and corporate managers, and Internet hosts, tend to be cowards. Afraid to deviate from the culture that rewards their cowardice. When challenged, they justify their cowardice with lies and character assassination.

Okay. I'd like to quote something you wrote: "We squander priceless opportunities to study ourselves and our living brains, as well as new ways to make us wiser, healthier and happier. We snuff out lives of criminals eager to make amends by donating their organs and helping science unlock some of nature's deepest secrets." Those are your words?

Yes. I also said that if there are willing condemned criminals, there must be willing non-criminals who have opted for euthanasia. I would perform the same experiments on those suicidal humans.

Are you talking only about physical disabilities, or do you include folks that are suicidal because of their mental condition?

If their suffering is primarily emotional and they have been unable to receive adequate care, then, yes, I would assist them. And, with their permission, I would experiment on them.

But isn't that immoral, Doctor?

What's immoral, and almost intolerably banal, is your moronic interrogation.

[Whistles, loud applause, one elaborate yodel]

The one word that's always used when talking about right to death campaigns is compassion. Would you describe yourself as a compassionate person, Dr. Death?

I'll leave those descriptions to others.

As long as they are not moronic, right?

Obviously.

Well, here is one of those others. And he is not moronic, even by your rigorous standards. A Nobel laureate in biophysics. He had this to say: "Whether Kevorkian's obsessions benefit humankind matters less to him than the rush—the almost orgasmic rush—he seems to get from handling and fantasizing about handling cadavers." Comment?

I already commented on sanitized scientists whose cowardice is rewarded. This so-called Nobel laureate is a prime example of that.

You are a very angry man, Doc. Don't you think that Dr Death here is an angry man, Charo?

Jes. But I like heem. He help people that don have no theen.

[Whistling, laughter, one raucous Bronx cheer]

You've got a fan, Doc.

I'm not an entertainer.

You're not? What about Slimmeriks and Demi-Diet? **To the Internet audience**: In 1975 Doctor Death authored a humorous diet book by that name. **To Kevorkian**: Wouldn't you call that entertainment?

Have you read the book?

Can't say that I have.

Read it. You might profit from it and extend your life. The gist of it, without the limericks, is don't smoke, avoid milk products, exercise moderately, eat as often as you need to, but only half the amount. Leave half of every plate uneaten.

That's it?

Basically. Without the humorous part—the limericks.

Can you recite one of those limericks for our virtual audience?

"A life of profane deglutition / Can end in a grave condition / How you consumed / Cannot be entombed / Thanks to the brave mortician."

[Puzzled laughter, mocking whistles, two ear-splitting Bronx cheers]

You hear that, Charo? Did you like Dr. Death's humorous limerick?

Jes. I do. Bery much.

Charo seems to be on your wavelength, Doc. Can't say that I am.

You may be soon if you keep eating, boozing, wearing that strong cologne, and obsessing about sex.

90

[Hoots, applause]

Give me a break! What do you have against sex?

Sex is sex. Obsessing about it or anything else will compromise your health. I wouldn't want you to die before your time.

But if I happened to drop dead you would harvest my organs?

Only with your permission.

[Loud, shrill, extended catcall]

Speaking of sex: You've never married. How come? Never found Ms Right? Or is there an issue—

My work.

Your work is death. You're married to death, is that it, Doc?

So are we all. You're an even bigger fool than I gave you credit for if you can't see that.

[pause]

Okay. Let's say euthanasia is finally permitted and becomes the law of the land. Would that satisfy you?

No. Such a death, no matter how serene, serves no constructive purpose beyond the bleak aim of extinguishing life.

You want to be able to conduct experiments on the corpses...

As I've been saying, I would conduct experiments on the cadavers and especially on the would-be cadavers, while he or she was still alive, but asleep of course, drugged beyond pain.

[Applause, two Bronx cheers, scattered yodeling]

Shoot. Looks like we've run out of time. Sorry about that, Doc. We have about thirty seconds. If you had a single word to say to our planet-wide virtual audience what would it be?

[Kevorkian does not respond]

Have you gone on Letterman yet?

Who?

David Letterman.

Glasses, gap-toothed, with the arrogant manner?

Er. That's him.

He's next. I think tomorrow. Need to check my calendar.

[pause]

Awesome. Well, that's a wrap. Doctor Death, it's been a…learning experience. You're a very, very interesting human. From now on, whenever I see that bumper sticker Death Sucks, I'll think of you in your funky cardigan and scuffed workshoes and be reminded that death, the big D, doesn't suck. It's us, the living-breathing folks, that, so to speak, suck death—and profit immeasurably from its grave restrictions.

Thanks a bunch, Doc. You're far from the dud I heard you were. You're a little weird of course, and sort of foul tempered, but you're actually a pretty cool guy. You've done it your way, and we all can appreciate that.

And you all out there in virtual land, from Pluto to Pensacola, from Uranus to Hyannis, from Tel Aviv to Texarkana, please give a little love to Doctor Death.

[Whistles, hoots, yodels, catcalls, loud applause, Bronx cheers, two or three shrieks of pain. Charo blows the doctor a kiss, which he does not acknowledge. He rises from the sofa, doesn't wave to the virtual audience, looks to the right, then left, which is where he heads, moving a little stiff-legged in his crewcut, plain shoes, ratty cardigan and Salvation Army trousers, offstage]

⊕Night Stalker⊖

After being sentenced and escorted from the courtroom in chains, the Night Stalker had to pass through a clot of reporters in their pee-stained boxers, fish ties and laptops.

One shouted: "How does it feel to be sentenced to death, Night Stalker?"

The Stalker smirked. "Death? Ain' no big deal.

"Comes wit' the territory.

"See you in Disneyland."

That Disneyland crack was cute.

Cute or acute?

Both. How'd you know about the pee-stained boxers? That would seem to be privileged information.

Supposition.

That like suppository? I know he had a thing for the anal cavity.

Ramirez?

Right. Ramirez. The Night Stalker.

Was the Stalker into the anal cavity? Yes, he was into the anal

94

cavity. About every male serial killer worth his salt is.

Why's that?

It's metaphysical. Plus that's where the funkiest action is reputed to be.

[pause]

Weapons of choice?

Machete and scalpel. When he was in a slashing mood.

Otherwise?

Had a .38 Smith, four-inch barrel. Had a butcher's cleaver. Had an ice pick. Had ropes, chains. Plus he'd use whatever was around. Situations dictated. He was a situational stalker.

He was resourceful?

Who's more resourceful than Satan? The Stalker had Satan looking over his shoulder.

Left shoulder or right?

Er, left.

Well, I have Smith Barney looking over my left shoulder. Reassuring in this volatile period. They're stock brokers.

I know what they are, foo'.

You're not a day trader, are you?

Negative.

[pause]

Let me ask you this: Manson in his prime or the Night Stalker? Who's more popular with the distaff side?

You kiddin' me. Ramirez drives fems crazier than Charlie Manson ever done. Had to unplug the phones from outside the holding tank after they nabbed him. Unplugged the fax. Disarmed the emails.

You're lying.

Plus they had a cordon of deps out front to keep the fems from breakin' on through.

Cordon of...

Deps. Fat-ass deputies cheek-by-jowl in riot gear. Was like the offensive line of the Oakland Raiders.

Just to protect the Night Stalker from his female admirers?

You kiddin' me. Was like fuckin' Elvis in his prime.

> **Fave music:**
> ***Heavy metal***
> **Fave sports:**
> ***X-games***
> **Fave actress:**
> ***Linda Lovelace***

Fave vacation spot:
Uranus
Fave food:
Women's feet

So what's your theory about why the Stalker gets 'em all sexed up? Latin eyes? Sunken cheekbones? The satanic mumbo-jumbo? That supple, skinny Mick Jagger bod?

Sunken cheekbones happen to look cool on TV. Latin eyes and a supple bod ain't gone hurt...

Flabass serial murderers don't make it on prime time, right?

Ain't that. It's how he done his murders. Check that. How the fems imagined he done 'em.

Scaled the roofs high above the sick asleep city.

Like a fly.

Climbed into bedroom windows while they slept their dreamless sleep.

Like a bat.

Super silent in his skintight jeans and Reebok hightops. Didn't make no noise a-tall.

Like a panther.

Black panther?

Thas right. Then he sprung. Then all the demon sounds of hell broke loose.

Screams, you mean?

More'n that. The Stalker unleashed a volley of sounds: howled, yowled, hooted, shrieked, bayed, sang…

How you mean, sang?

He had an excellent voice. You didn't hear about that? Tenor. When he'd be doing his shit—maiming, biting, cutting, whatever—he'd howl or bay. Then, when it came time for that anal cavity stuff you mentioned, he'd sing.

What would he sing? Opera? Blues? Reggae? Scat?

Scat.

> **Fave color:**
> *Red*
> **Fave hobby:**
> *Measuring coffins*
> **Biggest like:**
> *Coke on glass*
> **Biggest dislike:**
> *Money managers*
> **Make a wish:**
> *Have my middle finger on a nuclear triggering device*

So how many he nail? Ramirez. Final tally.

He started real simple, okay. Stomping, raping. Your garden variety serial killer. Young or old didn't matter. Dayle Okazaki and Maria

Hernandez were his first hits. Then came Tsa Lian Yu. Then Vince and Maxine Zazzara. After that, William Doi, Mabel Bell, Patty Higgins, Mary Cannon, Joyce Nelson, Chainaroung Khovanath...

Man, he was an equal-opportunity serial motherfucker. Did he have some kind of political correctness thing going?

Naw. Jus' doin' his shit. Those the kind of folks we have around these days. I guess you never heard of diversity.

I heard of it. He rape the dudes too?

Raped just the fems. According to the available evidence. Probably ended up offing twenty-eight, thirty. Left a bunch almost killed too. Good as dead, some of 'um.

[pause]

You said all them groupie fems wanted to break on through to get to the Night Stalker. What would they a done if they broke on through?

Tore him apart in their lust for him.

Like how do you mean?

Tear his arms, tear his eyes and telegenic sunken cheekbones, tear his sinewy hairless legs, his dick, tear the slick tongue out his head...Like they done to what's his name? Greek God down there.

Mercury?

One of 'em. Zeus, I think it was...

Dint folks eat their Gods in olden times?

Yeah. Fems woulda et him too. Fuckin' Night Stalker.

[pause]

You say they'd tear out his dick. Anyone ever see it to comment on?

What's that?

His dick. The dick of Richard Ramirez. Night Stalker.

You want to know about his dick?

Ain't that what it's all about?

He's uncut, average size, maybe a little bigger 'n average. Nothin to email your congressperson about.

Pity. A huge or even a tiny dick would have made a cool story.

Nah. Too hokey. The story's way cool the way it is.

So what happens after they et him? The adoring fems, I mean? They become sexier?

Exactly. They become silky, sexy night stalkers. Wear Lady Reeboks. Surprise males in their beds. Maim 'em with the ice pick and cleaver, fuck 'em, murder 'em…

Maim, fuck, murder. That the order Ramirez done?

That ain't all he done.

What else he do?

I ain't gone say. Not here. Not on the WorldWideWeb.

What do you look for in a gal?
Good ass, good legs
Perfect date?
Rum and sex at a cemetery round midnight
Describe yourself:
Motherfucker and proud of it
Motto you live by:
A corpse a day keeps the faggots away

You said he used a machete.

Machete and scalpel. The large and the small.

But then he would improvise, right? As the situation warranted. There was no set order of...mayhem?

Basically, you have two types of serial killer: calculated and spontaneous, which was the Stalker's M.O.

See. Now you got me all curious. What else is there besides maim, fuck, murder?

Use your own imagination.

Pierce, cleave, chop, chomp, stomp, plunder, blunder, rip, sever... I'm runnin' out of murderous adjectives.

That's your problem.

[pause]

I guess he came from a large family.

Uh-huh.

Born in Mexico, right?

Close. Texas. Near El Paso. Was the fifth of five children or the sixth of seven. Depending who's telling the tale. Around the age of 12, he started to hang with his cousin Jose, who'd been a Green Beret in 'Nam. Jose would show the kid Polaroids of rape, torture and mutilation he took in the war. Jose also taught young Richard how to fight to the death Green Beret style. Jose's wife Toni was alarmed at the shit Jose done during the war, and she didn't like the fact her husband did nothing but brag about his sexual brutalities and smoke pot all day long. One day Jose and Toni were arguing when Jose all of a sudden pulled out his Beretta 9, and shot Toni in the belly, killing her and splattering blood all over young Richard. Oh yeah, Toni was in her seventh month.

They say once you get an early taste of blood, it stays with you. So in a sense that was Ramirez's initiation?

Somethin' like that.

So what happened to his cousin? Jose?

First they tried anger management on him. When that didn't work they stuck him away. Nuthouse. Ended up offing himself.

Weapon of choice?

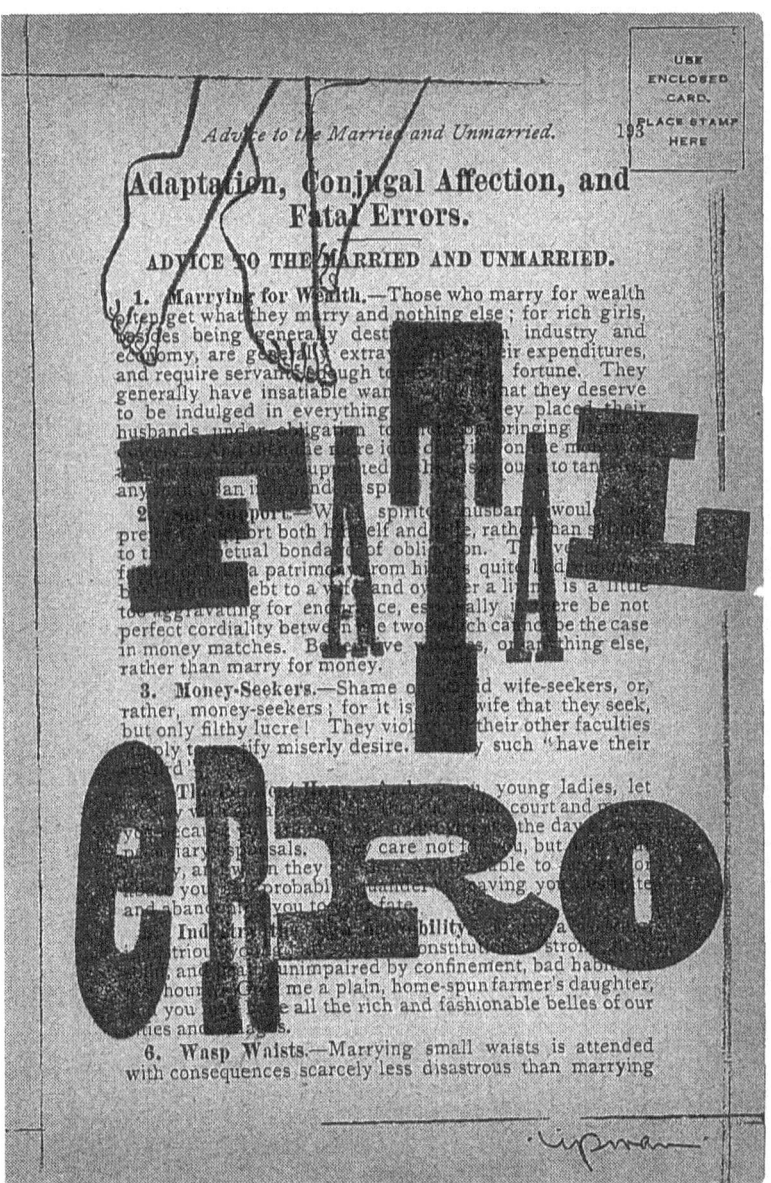

Underwear. Made a noose out of his jocks and tee shirt. Stuck his head in the makeshift noose…

Well, Richard Ramirez ain't so keen on himself either. Kept changin' his name. Rubin Cienfuegos, Noah Mimosa.

Julio Muertisimo, Hoagy Nalgas.

Hoagy Nalgas. That's cool.

You like it? Didn't cut him no slack from the judge. Sentenced him to death nineteen times.

You sure about that number? I heard fourteen.

[pause]

Lucifer is another name for Satan, right?

Uh-huh.

So did the Night Stalker actually make a pact with Satan or is he just yankin' our chain?

What do you think?

Don't make no dif to me. The Stalker's shit is freaky either way. Especially those last words he nailed them with when they led him away. I've got a copy stuck to my fridge. I read it, or some of it, every time I have a Spam sandwich and Bud Lite. From the bottle. Never use no glass with Bud Lite.

Since you know the Stalker's last words by heart why don't you recite it for our world-wide Internet audience.

When?

Right now, foo'.

> **You don't understand me.**
> **I am beyond your experience.**
> **I am beyond good and evil.**
> **I will be avenged.**
> **Lucifer dwells in all of us.**
> **I don't buy into the hypocritical, moralistic dogma of your so-called civilized society.**
> **You maggots make me sick.**
> **Legions of the night, night breed, repeat not the errors of the night prowler.**
> **Show no mercy.**

●Lonely Hearts●

Martha Beck was large, Ramon Fernandez was sleek. Martha, 41 (she said 35), was a mortician's assistant without rhythm. Ramon, 39 (he said 33), wore a hairpiece and was born to dance. That's an exaggeration; let's say he looked smooth and flashy on the dance floor, especially from a slight distance.

Martha was not graceless. Given her size and the fact that she lived and handled cadavers in Pensacola, Florida, she was light on her feet and smelled clean. To Ramon her lips smelled of strawberries, her red hair smelled freshly permed, and her pussy...her pussy was a bog. Peaty. Ramon like the smell of peat.

Martha would lick under Ramon's rubies (that's what she called them), and that musky-sexy smell was how he smelled all over, beneath his cologne. He wore *Grito*, by Almodovar. Yes, that Almodovar; he'd taken a sabbatical from movie making to establish his own line of fashion wear, which turned out to be fabulously successful. *Maricón* has the Midas touch.

Ramon wished he'd had the Midas touch. But that was when he was feeling sorry for himself. Hell, bilking 47 widows and spinsters of their savings wasn't all that shabby for a faded gigolo with a hairpiece, florid dance technique, tendency to migraines, and a big dick.

Ramon was born in Honolulu of Spanish parents. So he claimed.

They could have been Puerto Rican or Salvadoran, Cuban or Dominican. He did live in Spain for a time, near Málaga, married there, fathered three daughters, whom he deserted after the divorce from his Catalan wife. He escaped to Canada during the Vietnam conflict, came back after the war and chilled in New Orleans, where he studied black magic and reputedly got himself a Mojo hand. Somewhere along the way he decided he was irresistible to females.

Martha didn't mind washing and handling cadavers; truthfully, she liked it. What she didn't like were the smells of the toxic chemicals injected into the cadavers to stall decomposition. Plus her mortician boss was a dick. She managed to land another job for more money: assistant superintendent of a home for physically disabled children, also in Pensacola. Martha preferred corpses to noisy, needy kids, but was prepared to bend.

From New Orleans Ramon followed his penis, so to speak, east into the Florida Panhandle. Living there was relatively cheap, unattached fems were plentiful, and the tropical climate was good for his hormones. Ramon loved to sunbathe nude, though not without his hairpiece. This was before chlorofluorocarbons.

After three failed marriages, Martha advertised in the *Pensacola Tribune's* Lonely Hearts Club column, which just happened to be where cheetah Ramon stalked his wildebeests. Ramon contacted Martha and she invited him to call on her in her bungalow in Pensacola. They weren't together fifteen minutes before she led him to her queen-sized bed to rut. Noisy passion. Martha did all of the dirty talking. For Martha it amounted to love at first thrust; she found him irresistible.

Ramon, with the hair-trigger hard-on, found Martha surprisingly passionate for a very fat woman. And she didn't smell funky like other obese humans who can't get to all the holes and crevices to soap them thoroughly. Teaming up with a fat person was not on his agenda. Nonetheless, Ramon played his part and managed to introduce the question of money. Martha confided that she had amassed nearly thirty thousand dollars in savings, which was a strategic lie. She saw what he was up to and meant to cut him off at the pass.

They met and rutted the next night, after which Ramon "borrowed" $1500. He stayed away for four days, driving to Mobile to cultivate a blue-haired widow in that fair city. When he returned Martha was waiting in his apartment. Literally. She'd persuaded the janitor to let her in. The triumphant look on her face preempted Ramon's anger. She had read all of his letters from lovelorn females and even gone through his cancelled checks. Given that incriminating data, even a stupid person could have figured out Ramon's game, and Martha was the opposite of stupid.

Martha then made an offer that Ramon could not easily reject: They work as a team, she scour the lonely hearts' columns, they select the marks together. When Ramon called on the mark, she would travel with him disguised as his sister. Ramon didn't like any of it and especially that last craziness. He felt the beginnings of a migraine. The thought of murdering her flitted through his pounding head. Except he wasn't a murderer. He accepted her offer. The migraine abated. They rutted on Ramon's king-sized bed.

The first mark they did ensemble was a twice-widowed, sixtyish human called Faye Klug who lived in Tallahassee. She had advertised in the lovelorn column of the *Tallahassee Sentinel*, Ramon had responded, phone calls ensued, and now a visit was arranged. Swarthy sleek Ramon and his capacious older sister "Marta," wearing a black wig and "suntan" makeup, rented a Ford and drove east to Tallahassee, the tropical capital of the proud Sunshine state.

THE DEMI-WIDOW

"Quite! I like this young fellow here. And I like yo... nur... A... matter of fact, I was stand-ing th... ...g I might see you both again. I'm ...g myself your body-guard. Tomorrow morning at nine, I'll take on my new duties."

"Oh, but—but I don't know what to say, sir. I don't... kno... your name."

"My ...e... ...y yo... half... l ...sieur 'Milo. A... do... let' ...e al... t ... arrange-ment. It's ...l s... ed."

...ey finally took thei... eparture the baby wal... b...yard opening an... ...in... is fa...fist in a go...-by ... v... At ...orne... e a... Nina flut-tered ...fina... e be... ...ey ...ppo...d. As he watched them g... Car... o as... ...el... why he had ...there... ass... ...e the responsibility of... this un-kno... cl...? ... fo... ...ly the a...wer that ... was ... ab... ...ba... that... ...ad made ...ndous imp...

...it, he wondered, the little ...e... rm and friendly manner? Or was i... ...musing way his curls dipped jauntily forwar... ...his nose? Per-haps, it was his eyes: they were deep blue, almost

[166]

Gaunt and grey, wearing orthopedic shoes, the widow Klug appeared to like Ramon, but she clearly couldn't abide Marta. The siblings put up in her small tract home, and for the sake of propriety the widow shared a bedroom with sister Marta. If Ramon were solo he would have seduced the widow to hasten the process. But Marta, who proved to be fanatically jealous, insisted that Ramon not rut with any of the marks from then on. Less strong-willed than she, Ramon resentfully agreed. But sometime after two a.m. on the third night the widow Klug sneaked out of her bed and crept into the guest room and the bed of Ramon. They were a millimeter away from animal congress when a furious Marta burst in and hacked the widow to death with a cleaver she had providentially packed. The widow, on top (for the first time in her sensual life), bled all over the seducer Ramon.

Ramon bolted out of bed and into the bathroom dripping blood. He had never been involved with killing before and now he had a panic migraine. Marta tried to reason with him but he wouldn't leave the bathroom. Marta returned to the bedroom and carried the dead widow into the kitchen. She held Faye upside down and drained her blood, or most of it, into the kitchen sink. Next she laid the lean, bloodless cadaver on the cutting board and butchered her.

It took seven trash bags (industrial sized) to dispose of Faye Klug. The widow's orthopedic shoes, which had revolted Marta, she deposited in the seventh bag. She transported the trash bags to the widow's Oldsmobile in the garage. Then she thoroughly washed the bedding and floor. By the time she was finished there was no visible trace of the widow Klug. It was 5:15, nearly dawn. Ramon was still in the locked bathroom. Marta could hear his soft sobs through the door.

When Ramon finally emerged at 6:25, Marta was sipping coffee at the small table in the kitchen. He sat down next to her and she poured him a cup. Marta knew where the widow Klug had stashed her money, nearly $8000. They snatched the money, locked up the house and left for Pensacola at 7:20 a.m., Marta piloting the dead widow's Olds, Ramon driving the rented Ford.

Neither said anything about the murder. Both knew they had crossed the line. Ramon secluded himself in his apartment nursing his migraine.

Five or six days later Ramon moved in with Marta. A few days after that, Marta uncovered an ad in the *Panama City Pylon* from a 28-year-old widow with a four-year-old daughter living in Panama City. The widow was called Delphine Dearborn, and Marta sensed that she would have to be hawkeyed to assure that no sex transpired between her and Ramon. The photo the young widow subsequently sent confirmed Marta's anxieties; Delphine was almost beautiful. Why then did she advertise in the lonely hearts column? She was, she confided in her first letter, a born-again Christian who didn't drink, smoke, fornicate, blah, blah. In Marta's experience, pious Christians were the most corruptible.

Ramon and Marta boarded with Delphine in her stucco tract house just west of Panama City proper. While Ramon was courting the beautiful widow, Marta ingratiated herself into looking after Delphine's four-year-old child, Rainelle. She slept in a cot in the child's room. Ramon slept in the guest room. As usual, Ramon worked fast, and on the third day he'd gotten full disclosure re Delphine's savings.

The full disclosure may be attributed to what happened on the second evening. While they were all watching a musical variety show on television in the common room, Ramon got up and did his John Travolta-Saturday Night Fever routine. He was wearing tight shorts and looked sexy. When the widow Delphine awoke the next a.m. she was in love with him. The faded gigolo recognized the change in her and knew he had made his conquest. Now he wanted nothing more than to bed the gorgeous Christian, but how to escape the eagle eye of severe sister Marta.

Providence intervened: Marta woke up with a terrible toothache on the morning of the fourth day, which meant that she would have to drive to a dentist in Panama City. Obviously she was reluctant to leave, even for a few hours. She tried to persuade Ramon to accompany her, but he begged off claiming he felt the onset of a migraine. Marta was in too much discomfort to argue.

Ramon and Delphine seized the moment to rut in Delphine's double bed. Passionate, fiery even, the Christian was agile—almost acrobatic—which allowed Ramon to bust some moves he hadn't done since his enforced fidelity to Marta.

Marta returned some two-and-a-half hours later one tooth poorer. Immediately, she went into the widow's bedroom and smelled the sex. Ramon of course would deny it. He and the widow Delphine were sitting on the small porch making small talk. Meanwhile Rainelle was pulling at her "nanny" Marta's dress. The child wanted attention. Before she knew what she was doing, Marta slapped the brat hard across the face.

Screaming blue murder, Rainelle ran onto the porch. The evil blood-red splotch on her cheek told the tale, and the widow, clasping the wrist of the hysterical child, bounded into the house. Delphine ordered Marta to pack her clothes and leave her home. At once. After glaring at her, Marta went to her room. Ramon excused himself and followed her. In urgent whispers they discussed their options. Ramon argued that in two or three more days he'd gain access to at least some of the widow's savings. Clearly Marta had to leave, but not for home; she would hole up in Panama City, while Ramon continued to work his magic. With one condition, of course. No sex.

It was a condition Ramon had no intention of fulfilling. With the house locked against intruders (Marta), Ramon and the amorous Christian rutted long and often. The more they rutted, the more she seemed to crave it. In the dawn hours of the second night, after a marathon session of fornication, Ramon had a shower and retired to the guest room (They were sleeping apart in case Marta broke into the house at night and found them together.)

Ramon had removed his hairpiece and was settling into bed when the fervent Delphine opened the door without knocking and encountered him hairpiece-less. She was staring at him with a wild surmise when Ramon, livid, hurtled out of bed and lunged for her throat. He throttled her on the spot. She fell down dead at his feet. He snatched his hairpiece, dressed, slid into the widow's Buick Century and sped to Marta in Panama City.

Ramon and Marta returned to the house in the Century. The child was still asleep. Marta suffocated her with her pillow. Then the former mortician's assistant drained the blood from both bodies and butchered them. The full-bodied widow and child took up eleven trash bags which Marta and Ramon squeezed into the Buick Century. All they got their hands on was $187 from the widow's purse and from various drawers. If only Ramon had waited one more day. But he was irrationally, violently narcissistic about being caught without his hairpiece.

Did Marta know about the hairpiece?
Yes. She was the only other one.
Was Marta pleased that Ramon throttled the beautiful sex-crazed widow even without getting to her $$?
What do you think?

The Delphine Dearborn misadventure drove them even closer together. Their rutting was more passionate than ever. Repentant now, and scared, Ramon rutted like an adolescent diving into his mom. Marta liked that; she felt more secure. But house guests and fish start to stink after the third day; the grifters became restless. Ten days after misfiring with Delphine and Rainelle, they found themselves in Chattahoochee, FL, in the trailer home of a Creole widow named Prudence Lorena. Miss Prudence, going on seventy (she said 54), was part Chickasaw, African, Chinese, and Irish American. Like Ramon, she was dark complected and evidently saw at once that "Marta" was impersonating Ramon's sister.

Only Miss Prudence didn't let on that she saw. Either she was too smitten with Ramon to raise a fuss, or she was something of a grifter herself. For once, Marta turned her head and permitted Ramon to rut with the revolting old lady if that's what he chose to do. Interestingly, Miss Prudence, though on the brittle side, knew how to rut, and Ramon mostly enjoyed it. The odder thing happened *après* lust. Sharing a cigarette on their back in bed, Miss Prudence, appealing to his money-lust, tried to turn the gigolo against Marta. The old woman claimed she had access to $110,000 in savings, which she would share with Ramon if they murdered Marta and shacked up together.

Apparently Miss Prudence had gambled that even if Ramon turned down her offer and ratted to Marta, they wouldn't murder her without first getting to her money which was securely out of range. The prospect of murdering Marta and taking up with the old lady held no appeal for Ramon. Actually it gave him a headache. Marta saw that he was preoccupied and grilled him. He ended up divulging Miss Prudence's scheme.

What Marta and a reluctant Ramon decided was to murder the old whore never mind her shitty money. The idea was for Marta to get to her when she slept, except that Miss Prudence was not a sleeping kind of old woman. On the fourth night Marta had a go at it anyway. The Creole was lying on her back in her narrow bed when the fat but light-footed murderess crept into the room and raised the cleaver. Prudence veered and Marta ended up grazing her. Then Prudence fought back like a wildcat and actually seemed to be getting the best of it, when Ramon came up behind and smashed her on the head with a heavy skillet. He had to hit her several more times to shut her down. She bled a lot for a skinny, crusty old lady. Butchered, she amounted to four industrial sized trash bags, the fourth only one-third filled.

Marta and Ramon were back in Pensacola with nothing to show for it. Not only that, each of them, at about the same time, seemed to have lost all enthusiasm for the lonely hearts scams. One morning ten or so days after their fruitless return, they awoke around 8:30 and rutted with more than their customary passion. Something was in the air. While Marta was preparing the coffee, Ramon put on his hairpiece, took out his Smith & Wesson .38 Police Special, fitted a silencer onto it, went into the kitchen and shot Marta in the head from behind as she was standing at the stove. He dragged her body into the bedroom and laid it across the bed. Ramon couldn't kiss her face because it was in fair part blown away. He kissed her upper arm. Then, patting the top of his hairpiece, he shot himself in the chest and collapsed on top of her.

⊕Slick Ted⊖

Why did I make such an ugly corpse?

They fried me.

Fry Tyrone Power, fry Rock Hudson, fry Sly Stallone, and they'll come out plug-ugly, trust me.

Even if they embrace Jesus and denounce pornography at the 11th hour like I did.

As nuclear families go, mine wasn't that bad.

My mother, Eleanor, had poor taste in men but adored me.

My stepfather was a retired army cook who couldn't cook.

Couldn't bake either.

Johnnie Culpepper Bundy, known as Pep.

I loved my grandfather, he lived in PA.

Problem is we moved from there to Washington state when I was four years old.

Pep was into banging my mom, Eleanor.

Knocked her up four times, at least four.

Once I interrupted them, she was tummy down, he was straddling her.

Pep had the yardage, I'll give him that.

If he was my real dad I'd say I inherited that from him.

Tire iron in the jocks.

Me, I get the iron only when I'm peaking.

Other times I'm average.

Maybe even a little below.

Which is why my brief, brutish life has been wholly devoted to peaking.

It all started with the P-word: Pornography.

I'm getting ahead of myself.

My four step-brothers and sisters: I looked after them.

Babysat them, toilet trained them.

Inculcated the values of our great Christian democracy into them.

Good student, good manners, good looking: I did everything to a T.

So don't use that convenient "he came from a dysfunctional fam" bit on me.

I started getting funky only after I discovered porno.

That's not completely true.

There was a brief weird period when I was about 15.

I raped then whacked (actually it was the other way around) a young mark.

Neighbor girl who'd been following me around.

She was 12 or 13, can't remember her name.

Whacked her schnauzer too.

They never found the corpse.

Could be I did a few other things in high school.

But my porno addiction was the big impetus for going psycho and whacking the 40 or so that I'm famous for.

The reason why is Stephanie Brooks.

Stephanie Brooks' rejection drove me into the siren arms of Pornography.

This was at the University of Washington.

I'd gotten a scholarship to the U. of Puget Sound and transferred to UW the next year, majored in Chinese.

Why Chinese?

My first choice was Bengali, I wanted to work with Mother Teresa in Calcutta.

Minister to the poorest of the poor.

But those good intentions conflicted with golf, which was a passion.

I was just this far from being good enough to join the pro tour.

UW is where I met Stephanie, like I said.

From Palo Alto, old money.

I developed a crush on her and her old money, and she seemed to like me, think I was sexy, etc.

Only I made the mistake of moving too fast, on the second date I stuck my fist in her crotch, etc.

Which is what she wanted, only she didn't know what she wanted.

She reeled back from me like I was the devil.

Which got me to thinking that maybe I was.

Maybe that wasn't so bad.

Lovesick, I dropped out of college.

I'd already learned enough Mandarin to impress busboys in Chinese restaurants.

Never got me a free meal, though.

Never got me a bowl of Wonton.

That's the way the human race is, one reason I got into whacking them.

The other reason, like I said, was porno, accessed mostly in mags and seedy movie theaters.

Wasn't much video in those days.

My favorite was anal intercourse.

The very large in the very tight, hotly contested.

Also bondage, violent cross-dressing.

Tire iron in my jocks.

Straight razor in my fake leg cast.

Ice pick, rope, and cuffs in the glove compartment.

Crowbar under the driver's seat.

Porno got me buzzing, made me peak.

At the same time it weakened me.

It's hard to explain.

But I was still a Christian and a Republican, didn't change my politics one bit.

With the embrace of porno came wanderlust.

I loved to drive.

Especially the TransAm.

Let me tell you something: the tan VW bug worked even better, got me more marks.

They'd see this clean-cut, slick looking guy, white small teeth, slide out of the bug with his leg in a cast.

Irresistible.

Washington, Oregon, Utah, Colorado, Florida.

I whacked a couple of marks in NYC too, the Bronx.

Puerto-Ricans.

Maybe they were Cuban.

Hoes is what they were, which is how I treated them.

I always wanted to bite a nipple off in the burnt-out Bronx.

I had to be the only registered Republican in the whole scummy borough.

Visualize the scene: Slim, handsome, Caucasian Republican with his left leg in a fake cast slides out of his tan '63 VW Bug with that toothy smile and fat tire iron in his chinos in the burnt-out Bronx.

I'm getting ahead of myself.

After I dropped out of college and sank into violent porno I began to imagine playing the devil.

Whacked two young marks in Olympia in honor of my newly crowned anti-godhead.

Tammi and Joni I think they were called.

Long-legged and tan with blonde long straight hair parted in the middle.

Could've been Southern California transplants for all I know.

I lured them with the "broken" leg.

Lumped them with the crowbar.

Did the very large in the very tight deal with the tire iron while biting off some nipples.

Joni's was pink and puffy, Tammi's large and brown with broad aureoles.

Joni's tasted sweet and sticky, Tammi's tasted pickled.

Slit their throats and dropped them in one of our wooded areas.

Washington is a green state.

Compensation of sorts for the continual rain.

I drove back to Seattle and did the unexpected.

Re-enrolled in UW, majoring this time in Political Science, with an eye on the Law.

Using my slick looks and soft sell I gained entry into high-level Republican circles.

The same gifts that got me into the panties of young, soon-to-be-dead marks, propelled me into the inner circle of the Republican Party.

What I noticed at once is that upper-echelon boardrooms stink way worse than any sodomized, bludgeoned, headless, decomposed mark.

There's a moral in that.

I said headless because I severed the heads of my Washington and Oregon kill and buried them up on Taylor Mountain near Seattle.

My range extended through Washington down into Oregon and Utah.

Utah turned out to be a mistake because that's where they collared me.

I was enrolled in the University of Utah law school.

Mormons on every side of me.

I'd already whacked seven or eight in and around Salt Lake City.

Then I got a grip on this young Mormon mark with glasses, but when I tried to cuff her in the bug she slipped away and fell out the door.

Should have followed my first impulse which was to pass on her.

I never liked marks with glasses.

She had a weird name, Carol DaRonch.

She got away, but not without some bite marks on her shoulder.

Bite marks is how they collared me.

Mormons will take multiple wives but not bite them.

Me, I was a biter.

Only it got worse after I discovered porno.

Meg Anders, who I lived with for five or six months in Seattle then dumped, testified against me in court.

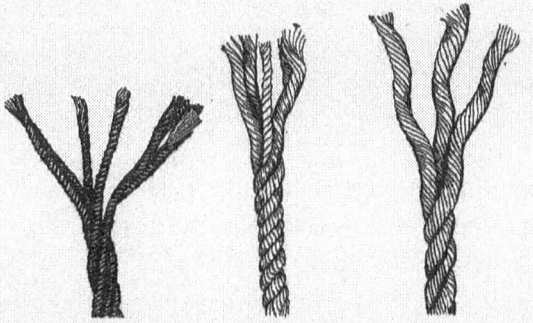

HOUSE PAINTING METHODS

much to be preferred because they carry much
r loads nd so the factor of safety is greater.
ng Stage Falls, e ro es may
be had in a en and on gh grade should
be used,—th is place to e mize. Ma rope
is most com nly sed. Si l ro sa The
best grade o an rope wi safely carr hes ads:

⅝ inch —4,00 nds
¾ inch rope—4,700 pounds
⅞ inch rope—6,5 pounds
100 f ⅝ in ope wei s about 13 ds
10 eet of ¾ is pe wer about po ds
100 ⅞ ch e wei s about pounds

Ro are ect to iati in quality ame
as other merchandise and it is not safe to buy "just
ropes." Know what kind and quality you are buying

Plate 81.—Swing Stage Rope Falls

and eal on resp ble dealers an manufac
tur
M re h which oo rope n e is ot
all the me h quality Al there e struc-

lipman

Said she saw plaster of Paris and a partial leg cast in my room.

Found a butcher's cleaver, ice pick, rope, and handcuffs in my bug.

Said I kept pornography and wanted to play rough sex with her and bite her titties and genitalia.

Carol DaRonch also picked me out of a lineup.

The Mormons jailed me.

Then they transferred me from Salt Lake City to Garfield County Jail, in Rifle, Colorado, population 4,237.

Human beans—more than you'd think—wrote to me in prison and asked what exactly I did to the marks before or even after whacking them.

Wanted all the sexy, gory details.

I did everything you fantasized me doing to them.

And more.

Wanted to know what made me choose one mark over another?

Iron in my jocks.

When it peaked I got to whacking.

Why did I sever their heads and bury them up on Taylor Mountain?

No particular reason.

I broke out of Garfield County Jail through the prison kitchen.

There's no way Rifle, Colorado is capable of holding Ted Bundy against his will.

Six days later they collared me in Aspen.

I escaped again three weeks later, this time through the ceiling.

Cold weather is boring if you don't ski.

A college town in the sun with lots of marks was what I craved.

Florida State University, Tallahassee.

First I stopped in Chicago.

Business or pleasure? Pleasure.

I whacked myself a brace of young marks.

No false leg routine this time.

Just broke into their dorm suite and got cracking.

When I got to Tallahassee I rented a studio apt near the University.

Called myself Johnny Culpepper, which was just another name, no symbolism intended.

For a few hundred dollars I bought myself a used bug, kelly green.

Surveyed the city, especially around the university.

Saturday night late, Chi Omega Sorority house.

Most of the coeds out partying, but some left behind: wallflowers and a few good lookers pining for their absent boyfriends.

I wasn't into wallflowers.

Ugly people hurt my eyes.

Made me want to vomit, which is something I hate to do.

Maybe I should have waited for a weekday night when the beds were filled with prime-time coeds.

Only that tire iron in the jocks—it couldn't wait.

I made my move at 1:45 a.m., slipped into a corridor window on the first floor.

Weapons?

Tapered oak log with a torn-away sleeve from my blue terry cloth robe wrapped around it.

Straight razor, ice pick, rope, and rags.

I wore a black mesh stocking mask.

Two of the five bedrooms on the first floor were locked, two were empty, the fifth contained a "wallflower" asleep and snoring in her bed.

I scampered to the second floor.

The first bedroom was locked, but the one next to it was open, and when I shined my light: sweetness.

Two slim marks asleep on top of the covers in a single bed, the blonde wearing bikini panties, the redhead nothing at all.

I bludgeoned the blonde with the oak then stuck the rag down the red's throat before she got her scream half-out.

Bound her to the bed so she could watch me ass-fuck her dead and bloody lesbo lover.

Then I retied the red so that I could strangle her while ass-fucking her with the fat crown of the "tire iron" coated with her lesbo lover's dung.

First I did some biting.

I got the second load off even faster than the first.

Slit both their throats just to make sure they were goners.

Believe it or not, I had a couple or three loads left, maybe more.

Serial killers are like stunt dicks in porno loops.

Except what I did could not be undone.

Which was fine with me.

Serpent spitting fire, I slinked up to the third floor.

Again the first bedroom was locked, but the one to its left was open.

When I shined the light, the bed was unmade but empty.

Just then a toilet flushed and a mark came out of the small bathroom.

She saw me at the door and screamed and then I whacked her.

No time to ass-fuck her.

Loud, agitated voices in the corridor.

I opened the door and took off.

At the stairs a mark reached for my head and came away with the mask.

I was out of there, in the bug.

Less than a mile or so east of the sorority house I spotted a mark in an upstairs window and veered into a parking spot.

Then I saw that I'd left the straight razor at the first place.

Big mistake

But psychopaths are not going to think when they're hot.

My iron was working.

I jimmied the outside lock, bound upstairs and knocked at the door.

Wasn't sure what I'd do if someone besides the mark answered, but the mark answered.

"Wha…" is all she said.

Then and forever.

I stuffed the rag in her mouth.

We were on the floor.

I whacked her with the log, but when I went for her nipples saw that she was flat as a board.

For a second I thought she was a fag.

But no, she had a cunt and asshole.

I did her on the floor.

Tight fit all around.

For a fresh kill especially.

Can't recall ever dropping that large a load.

Mark's phone was ringing.

Glanced at my watch: 3:40 a.m.

Sort of late to call, even in cosmopolitan Tallahassee.

Could be someone spotted me whacking her through the window.

I got out of there fast and into popular history, sordid, made for TV.

Interfacing with sharks and Nazis and rattlesnakes.

Condemned and consumed by the vast American public.

Swallowed the way I swallow a whacked mark's pee.

Back in the bug I did something unforgivable.

Got into a fender-bender with an old guy in a Studebaker on a side street.

Had to get away on foot.

Spotted a black TransAm double-parked with the door unlocked.

Had a gold racing stripe just like my old TransAm.

I slim-jimmed the ignition, pulled onto the highway.

I'd been in the TransAm less than ten minutes when a cop car started flashing me.

I sped up and veered off the highway but the TransAm didn't have the juice.

Had to ditch the TransAm and hoof it.

The cop shouted a warning then shot eight times fast.

I fell, pretending I was hit…when he moved over me I wrestled his gun away.

But now one, then two, three radio cars, lights flashing, sirens burping, zigzagged to a stop in front of me.

I dove on the pavement and fired the cop's Colt, but there were only two rounds left in the magazine.

They collared me.

You recall that I went on to plead my own case in court, right?

Three separate trials in three years.

Got to use my law school theatrics.

Remember: I was always a straight-A student between whackings.

Naturally I had to wear a suit or sports jacket, which I wore unbuttoned.

Did you happen to steal a look at my crotch?

Jurors saw it.

Judges saw it.

This one old judge in the Chi Omega trial had his mouth open the whole time.

Every once in a while his coated old tongue would slip out and loll wetly over his thin chapped lips.

Like a horny old hound dog.

The reason why is I was showing yardage, sticking way out through my pants.

Fat, inflamed tire iron.

Sweet as can be.

Was it as sweet as whacking a mark?

No. No way.

But here's something I've lived by: if you can't get delirious, settle for second best.

Which for me was whacking forty-plus marks then arguing my case in court with a killer hard-on.

● Starkweather ●

Pack up a suitcase, babe.

How come?

Go for a ride.

Where to?

Go to New York. The Big Apple.

I don't want to go to New York.

Kalifornia, then. San Francisco. Flower Power.

What do we do for wheels? Money?

Snuff your hokey dad. Take his Chrysler and his money. Take his Rolex.

His IBM clone powerbook?

I got my own powerbook, babe. Got my own palm-pilot.

What about my mom?

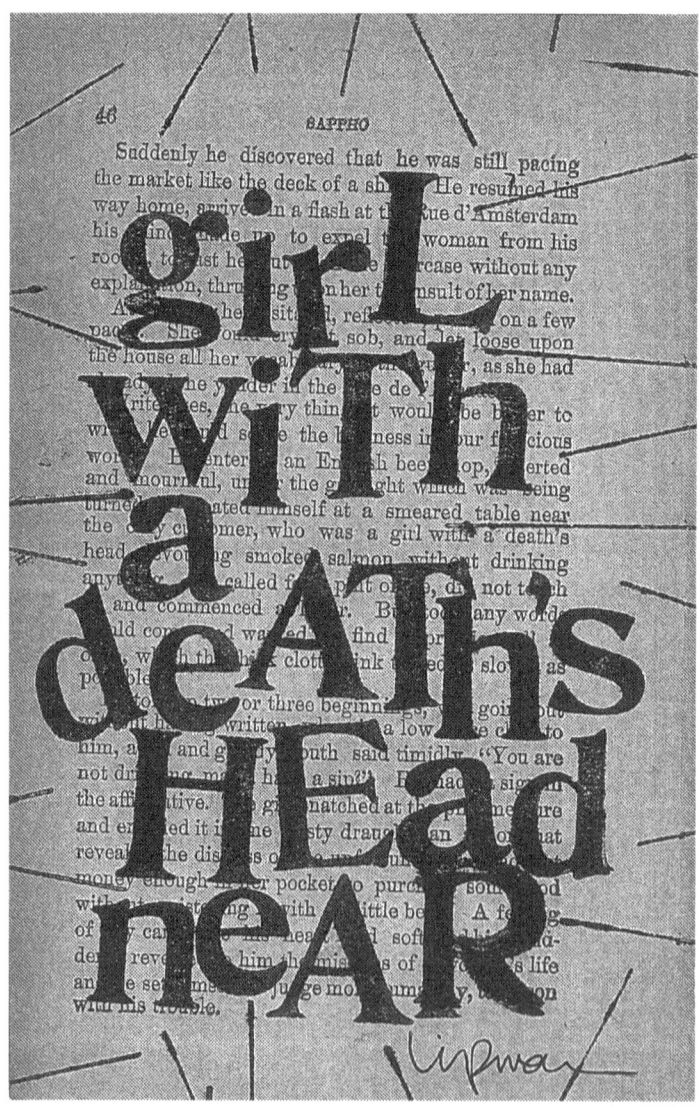

Snuff her. Take her nightie and shit.

Wear it when we sex?

Absolutely.

What about my dog? Muffin?

Take Muffin with us.

She don't like to ride in Chryslers.

So we leave her. Drop her at Josie's.

I'll miss her.

Josie?

Muffin.

We'll be back.

When?

When we're done.

Done…

Joy riding. Snuffin' hokeys. Having some fun.

How about sex?

That too. In your hokey mom's nightie.

Me on top?

Maybe. Depends how many we snuff.

What if they nail us?

Remember that last scene in Bonnie and Clyde?

Shot to shit in slow-mo.

Exactly.

Ton of bullets.

Mo' the better. You gotta go, go real fast.

Not me. I wanna savor. A single 9 mm round to the fat of the thigh. Bleed to death sweet and slow.

Your thighs are firm not fat, babe.

When do I get to wrap them around your neck?

Soon's we snuff us some hokeys. Get that old blood squirting.

How many we plan on doing like that?

Got to be double figures.

How come?

Get our ass on TV, the Internet. Wouldn't you like to see your sweet ass on the Internet

Yeah. Let's do 16.

16, 19. Who knows? We could do 23.

I like 16. My favorite number is 8 times 2.

Whatever.

When do we leave?

Sooner the better. Tonight.

I thought we gonna sex tonight.

We'll sex in the Chrysler. On the way to Kalifornia. After we snuff your hokey folks.

If we sex while we drive you won't be able to wear my mom's nightie.

Sure I will. Look at what's stuck in my jeans.

Smith 357.

Got me 3 more.

All Smiths?

Hell no. Got me a Glock and 2 Sigs. 9 mm.

I bet you stole them.

[Starkweather grins]

Charlie Starkweather! You stole them, didn't you?

Forgit it. It's a guy thing. You ain't a guy.

I'm glad you noticed. Sometimes I wonder.

What you wonderin' 'bout, little darlin'?

If you like me. If you even like girls.

I like gals when I'm snuffin' hokeys. When I ain't I could care less.

That's what we're gonna do, right? Snuff hokeys?

Fuck yeah. All the way to Kaliforn-I-A.

I'm expectin' some real hot sexin' from you, Chuck.

You got it, babe.

You in my mom's bloody nightie and padded bra.

You in your dad's Rolex and Texas boots.

The boots he wears to line dance with?

Those exact ones. What time you got?

Ten till.

Your hokey dad must be home from his job in the korporation.

They're eating dinner.

What they eatin'?

Today's Wednesday? London broil.

Does your hokey dad remove his korporate nametag when he eats his London broil?

Sometimes yes, sometimes no.

Let's go snuff us some hokeys.

Should I pack a suitcase first or after?

First. So we split real quick. I copped the Glock for you. Lightweight stocks. Easy to handle. Want to snuff your mom or your dad?

Mom.

Why did I have a feeling you'd say that?

What about Muffin?

Drop Muffin off at Josie's on the way to the superhighway.

Josie don't live near the superhighway.

So we drop the pup and double back. No biggie.

[Pause]

Chuck.

What, darlin'?

What if I don't like Kalifornia?

Then we go on to Utah. Idaho, where all them white-is-beautiful folks is at. It's a big damn country.

Can't we just stay in Jersey?

Jersey sucks, babe. You know that. Ain't you curious about the rest of this humongous fingerfuckin' country of ours?

Not really.

oK & Ko

A long-awaited prison psychiatrist's report on Theodore Kaczynski was released Friday, graphically detailing the Unabomber's fantasies about mutilating a former girlfriend, murdering technicians, and having a sex-change operation.

A long-awaited judgment on the sexually deviant immigrant writer Jerzy Kosinski's literary merit will be delivered before the end of the performance.

Barring distractions and dead-ends.

Kosinski, now virtually forgotten, was the author of *The Painted Bird*, *Cockpit*, *Pinball, The Devil Tree*, and *Being There*, among other critically acclaimed sex-centered novels in the anything-goes Sixties and Seventies.

Kosinski committed suicide in 1991.

The 123-page report, compiled in part from interviews with Kaczynski in his Sacramento County Jail cell while he was heavily sedated, and from his alleged writings dating to his graduate student days at Harvard in the Sixties, states that Kaczynski's frustrated desire for a sex-change operation set him on the path to being a serial killer.

Kaczynski claims to have considered mass instead of serial murder but rejected it because of its (his own words) "excessive immediate gratification."

As an ascetic, even masochistic, revolutionary wannabe, gratification was way low on Kaczynski's list of cool things to feel.

The 123-page judgment, compiled from interviews with friends (few) and free-loaders (numerous), suggests that young Jerzy, while investigating his own body in his native land, may have uncovered a fresh erotic point of entry. Neither precisely anal nor vaginal, the entry was reportedly in the area of the perineum, a closed circuit, hence separated from sexually transmitted disease and unwanted pregnancy.

(This is not a metaphor.)

The young Pole knew at once that he had unearthed a unique, perhaps even revolutionary, sexual modality, but he could not find another human who took his discovery seriously, let alone anyone with whom to discuss it.

That lack of a significant other may well have contributed to his recreational drug use, gender slippage, and ensuing suicide.

Kaczynski allegedly wrote that his 1968 visit to a Beverly Hills psychiatrist to obtain official permission to become a female was a major turning point in his life.

Nineteen sixty-eight was a banner year for student revolutionaries world-wide, though not for Kaczynski.

After the psychiatrist flatly rejected his plea for sex-change surgery, he glared at her, first uncomprehendingly, then menacingly, finally bolting out of her office, pent up, consumed with "a visionary new hatred," according to youthful K's psychiatrist, Dr. Luanne Ortiz-Koontz, in her just-released, unauthorized biography: *I, Me, Mine: The Life and Times of Ted Kaczynski, Unabomber.*

Kosinski allegedly wrote that once in the Cold War late Fifties he traveled from Lódz, Poland (his birthplace) to Czechoslovakia, and while in Brno (birthplace of Freud, two-and-a-half hours from Prague) he witnessed an orgy with seven participants: two females, two F2M pre-op transsexuals, two gender-fast males, and a mongoose.

One of the pre-ops was a neo-Nazi and both decisive males were Gypsies.

Bodily fluid emissions and extreme violence were featured in the orgy, which mightily impressed the young Kozinski and would influence his writings indelibly.

What sorts of emissions?

You name it.

What sorts of violence?

Cutting, stabbing, branding, maiming, severing…

Did the mongoose figure prominently in the orgy?

Yes, prominently.

"Like a phoenix, I burst from the ashes of my despair," Kaczynksi was to write after partially recovering from the rejection of his request for sex-altering surgery.

"My very hopelessness liberated me because I no longer cared about death. Now I really could break out of my rut and do things that were daring, irresponsible, criminal, demented. If fools construed my wanton violence as having an ideological basis, so much the better.

"Obviously they will label me mad, because 'mental health' is defined by the extent to which a human behaves in accord with the needs of the system without showing signs of stress.

"And stress has always been my calling card."

"Like a phoenix, I burst from the ashes of my despair," Kosinski was to write. "After witnessing the brutally bloody mongoose orgy in Brno I was no longer swimming against the current. I was in fact coasting downstream, writing as effortlessly as emitting gas.

"I was the avant-garde's current darling, freshly rich, but still Jewish, tumescing while spelunking the southern (anatomically speaking) regions with a ballpoint pen in my teeth.

"Uneven, discolored, they were, alas, still Eastern European teeth.

"I hadn't yet made my fateful appointment with Zuck, the cosmetic dentist-to-the-stars of Beverly Hills."

Dr. Ortiz-Koontz's report on Kaczynski's 1968 visit, underwritten by a grant from the pharmaceutical industry giant, Eli Lilly, and sealed since January in U.S. District Court in Sacramento, was released Friday. Dr. Ortiz-Koontz, retained by the prosecution as a star witness, initially diagnosed Kaczynski, a former Harvard doctoral student, Berkeley mathematics professor, and backwoods hermit, as a paranoid schizophrenic.

She reaffirmed that diagnosis under oath, testifying that his paranoid schizophrenia had become "exacerbated" since 1968. Nonetheless, he was, Ortiz-Koontz insisted, fully competent to stand trial.

The initial diagnosis of 1968 is included in her new book, the sales of which have been "steady but moderately disappointing," according to Dottie Lowenthal, spokesperson for Ortiz-Koontz's publisher, Harper Collins.

"Serial killing in the US is a weekly ritual, and Americans have notoriously short memories," Lowenthal explained. "It could be they've forgotten all about Kaczynski and turned their attention to this week's serial or mass murderer.

"The intention of Dr. Ortiz-Koontz's book is to remind readers that the Unabomber was far different and a great deal more dangerous than your standard brand lunatic."

Dr. Ortiz-Koontz's report, underwritten by a grant from the pharmaceutical industry giant, Pfizer, and sealed since January in U.S. District Court in Washington, was released Friday.

Forensic psychiatrist Ortiz-Koontz, retained by the prosecution as a star witness, diagnosed Kosinski, a former compulsive wanker and sometime sociologist in his Polish homeland, as both a pornographic writer and paranoid schizophrenic, while insisting that he was fully competent to stand trial on his shoplifting charge.

May 1982, 10:50 a.m.: The famous, decadent Polish-American novelist Jerzy Kosinski, stoked, and possibly crazed, after a night of drinking champagne and freebasing cocaine, is alleged to have stolen

a robin's-egg blue sports bra and matching pair of terrycloth thong panties and leg warmers from Victoria's Secret in the pricey Barbarella Mega-Mall, just north of Santa Barbara.

If Kaczynski wished to be female why did he grow a beard, talk in a gruff voice, hole up in a cabin in the Montana outback, hunt his food with a bowie knife, and bathe only on Leap Year?

The answer, according to Hawley P. Guilford, Professor of Clinical Psychology at American University, is that "Ted strove to reject his unappeasable ideal (to become a female) by acting like an exaggerated version of a male."

The Unabomber's "contrary" response is not at all unusual, Professor Guilford added, and even has a technical name: "reaction formation."

If Kosinski wished to be female why was there so much macho gesture-making and penis brandishing in his pornographic novels?

One expert for the prosecution, Hoy P. Guilford, Professor of Clinical Psychology at Pacific Rim / Google, testified that "largely because of his ingestion of illicit drugs," Kosinski's libido became compromised while he was in his early thirties; as a result, "he reverted back to a sexualized version of the passivity of his childhood, when his Polish-Jewish parents dressed him as a little girl and lavished affection on him."

This was of course before the Polish-Jewish parents were captured by the Gestapo and transported to Auschwitz where life abruptly devolved into: *This vay to the gez, ladies undt gentlemen.*

Regarding his infamous *Unabomber Manifesto*, Kaczynski, under arrest and heavily sedated, revealed that it was a "cipher": ostensibly a call for an ethical revolution arrived at through a painstaking socio-historical analysis of virulent technology.

In fact—if one were to tease out the various subtexts—his manifesto was nothing less than a clarion call for sexual terrorism and cultural demonizing which targeted our most venerable American institutions.

Regarding his infamous, best-seller *Cockpit*, Kosinski, in an unguarded moment, revealed that his original title, *Negligee*, had been vetoed by his publisher.

Cockpit actually was authored by two male ghostwriters, one of whom was serving three life sentences in Attica for murder and was the proud possessor of two y chromosomes.

The cash profits were divided between Koskinski and his publisher.

For his contribution to the novel, the yy-chromosome ghostwriter had one of his three life sentences officially deleted.

The other ghostwriter was mysteriously pushed to his death into a southbound subway train during morning rush-hour on 96th Street and Broadway.

Penal experts are at odds as to whether the forcible ingestion of anti-psychotic drugs, shock treatment, psycho-surgery, and solitary confinement will reform the Unabomber.

But even the doubters concede that with execution for his federal crimes no longer a possibility, there needs to be some approved way of punishing him severely.

"Judas Cradle," "Heretic's Fork," "Knee Splitter," "Rectal Pear," and "Spiked Necklace" have each been cited as an appropriate mode of condign punishment.

Ethical torture, if you will.

After all, Kaczynski maimed or murdered in cold blood our bravest and best captains of industry.

Penile experts are at odds as to whether Kosinski's steady ingestion of non-prescription mind-altering drugs alone accounted for his gender erosion and subsequent impotence.

Or whether his debauched writing, social pessimism, and peacock gesture-making were contributing factors.

Would he still be alive and unambiguously male if Viagra had been available? Very likely.

However that kind of speculation is a further waste of taxpayer dollars. Because hindsight is infallibly twenty-twenty.

Reader-scanner, here, as promised, is the definitive judgment on Jerzy Kosinski's literary merit:

Compared, as he must be, to the great Polish-Anglo writer Joseph Conrad, Jerzy Kosinski is unlike…

Uh-oh, we've just experienced another one of those "rolling blackouts."

That's what we get for our passive reliance on monopolistic power. Corporate energy enforced by corporate government.

Reader-scanner, if you despise the servitude imposed by technology and its affiliates you can either roll over pretending it doesn't exist. Or you can remedy the situation.

First, we work to heighten the social stresses within the system to weaken it sufficiently for a revolution against it to become possible.

Second, we propagate an ideology that validates life and what remains of wilderness, while militantly opposing technology and the industrial state.

Such an ideology will assure that when the industrial-technological state collapses, its dehumanizing remnants will be smashed, bashed, shattered, crushed, pulped, pulverized, atomized, eviscerated, obliterated.

If, in some revolutionary future, you need to find me, look for me under your bootsole. I—or something of me—will be pulsing in the dirt and grass.

I said grass, not astroturf.

Never, ever astroturf.

☉ Speck ☉

It is the fateful summer of '66.

The Manson murders, which would symbolically mark the end of an era, are three years away.

Richard Speck is 24-years-old and intimately familiar with violence, drugs, alcohol and sexual abuse.

His mother, Lettie, had shacked up with Texan ex-con Carl Lindberg and moved her family of eight from Kirkwood, Illinois, to Dallas.

When Lindberg wasn't sodomizing Speck and his siblings he was slapping them around.

Speck's own marriage breaks up when his wife Glenda, a street cleaner's daughter, betrays him with a shaved-head acromegalic giant named Barney.

Glenda is herself large, six-feet-two, 212 pounds.

She wears a size-13 shoe and has thighs as wide as an ingenue's waist.

Her thighs would lock vise-like around Speck's back or neck when they rutted.

Which was less frequent than she wanted.

On the other hand, pock-faced Speck, 6-1, 153 in his socks and jocks, was bony in all the wrong places.

With broad hips and stick-out ears.

He emitted an unappealing odor, like sauerkraut gone bad.

Or five-day-old vomit.

He had less hair on his body than Glenda.

What he had in bed was a hair trigger, no staying power.

Speck found Barney and Glenda *in flagrante delicto* on the carpeted floor of their living room.

Check that: it was the *only* room—besides the cramped airless bathroom—in the South Side basement apartment.

To clear space for the gargantuan coupling they'd pushed the furniture against the walls.

Speck smelled 'um before he seen 'um.

A thick smell like sodden black earth shoveled into an open hole with something sour in the mix.

The fornicators may or may not have noticed Speck shuffling into the room.

Hell, it wasn't like the acromegalic giant was the only one.

Speck and Glenda would get drunk in local bars and return with one or two other drunken males.

Glenda would rut with the males while Speck watched.

When they rolled off her it would be his turn.

But after doing Barney the acromegalic giant Glenda didn't want any more of her lawfully married husband.

Speck worked in a Chicago boatyard until July 10, 1966, when a fight with a ship officer cost him his job.

The ship officer was getting the best of it, kicking and stomping Speck, when his heavy shoe connected with Speck's ear and knocked him senseless.

While Speck was crumpled and semi-conscious on the pavement the ship officer was reported to have spit then said:

"Your sorry ass is history.

Get the fuck out right now."

Which Speck did, after first borrowing money to buy booze and speed.

He rode the bus to a bar under the El called Skuggs and got started fast with slugs of Jim Beam and Coca Cola chasers.

Slouching at the far end of the bar away from the three or four other drinkers.

He returned to Skuggs for the next three days around 10:30 a.m., quitting twelve hours later.

On July 13, when he left Skuggs at 10:28 p.m., he was both drunk and stoned.

He'd injected a drug of some kind into his left thigh.

It could have been a speed compound.

It could have been cut with Sani-Flush.

Speck must have injected the drug into his thigh when he went to the john, which he did seven or eight times between 10:30 a.m. and 10:28 p.m.

Some forty-nine minutes later, stoned from the speed injected into his thigh and drunk from a few dozen bolts of Jim Beam Coke, Speck, armed with a snubnosed Ruger .38 and a foot-long butcher knife, knocks on the door of a townhouse called the Jeffrey Manor, a student nursery home attached to the South Chicago Community Hospital.

Knocks four times.

It takes sixteen seconds for the door to open.

Those are the same sixteen seconds that Saint Sebastian, bound to a Poplar, waits while his tormenters load their arrows.

The same sixteen seconds that Joan, in her altered state, waits for the pyre to flame.

Demure twenty-three-year-old Corazon Amurao opens the door wearing her nurse's uniform.

Though there is evidence that Speck scoped out the residence on at least one earlier occasion, he seems surprised that the girl is Oriental and that the Oriental girl is a nurse.

He waves his Ruger at her.

"I ain' gwine hut you," he says in a low drawl.

"I need yo money is all.

"I've got to git to N'Orleans."

Mass murder experts have speculated whether Speck really meant to go to New Orleans, and for what reason.

One theory is that while in the Merchant Marine brig, an African-American fellow prisoner named Luther ("Lowboy") Antoine informed Speck about the Mojo, which has to do with witchcraft and voodoo traditions.

The idea is that this Mojo, accessible only in Louisiana, would maybe improve Speck's shitty luck.

Speck gwine tuh Looziana git hissef a Mojo hand.

To the demure Cora, just five-feet-one in her white nurse's uniform, Speck, looking down, says in his Texas drawl:

"I ain' gwine hut you.

"I'm on'y gone tah you up."

Which he does, using the butcher knife to cut strips of bedding, gagging her as well.

Next Speck shuffles through the house, quietly, looking around, smelling the smells.

Finds six more girls, several in their nurse's uniform, three of them Oriental, and ties and gags each of them with bedding strips.

In the next forty minutes three more girls, one Oriental and two white, return home from dates and Speck ties and gags them.

There are a lot of beds in the large house.

The house possesses a smell he cannot place.

Could be the food they eat.

Or something else maybe having to do with their bodies.

It is a full moon night.

None of the girls, it appears, resists his tying them up, or even raises her voice.

So Cora Amurao, the sole survivor, would testify in court.

Mass murder experts have speculated on their apparent passivity.

The full moon, the girls' race (five were Filipinas), and the prospect of having found the ghoulish Speck sexy, have all been cited.

A few experts have even suggested that Cora was lying under oath.

Perhaps psychologically to separate herself from her close friends so brutally murdered.

Nine female nursing students, including five Filipinas, are in the fated townhouse in South Side, Chicago at thirty-four minutes after midnight on July 13, 1966.

After binding and gagging each of them with strips of bedsheet, Speck deposits them on the wood floor of the sitting room on the lower level.

Speck has pocketed all the money he could find, about ninety three dollars.

But he doesn't leave.

He turns on the TV in the sitting room, according to Cora's testimony, and watches the "Late Show" for twenty minutes or so, chain-smoking Camels.

It is a comedy of some kind.

Possibly Abbott and Costello.

Cora remembers Speck laughing a raucous, high-pitched laugh.

Abruptly, he turns off the TV.

Then he turns it on again, evidently as a sound shield.

He seems to have become agitated.

He leads a pair of girls to another room in the house where he stabs and strangles them.

Cora can hear the groans and occasional muffled screams above the TV noise.

After about an hour he returns to the main room, bloody, and this time leads a single girl into the killing room.

Cora claims to have heard him say to this girl, Linda DeMarco, "Would you mind putting your legs on my back?"

He takes his time, disposing of about one girl per hour.

When, hours later, Speck comes back for yet another turn, Cora has rolled herself under a bed out of sight.

She lies there silently and watches Speck push her close friend, the bound and gagged Gloria Davy, on top of the bed under which she—Cora—is hidden, and rape her.

Cora, hunched on her side, feels every one of Speck's thrusts on the thin mattress above her.

Not having any staying power, Speck penetrates and squirts rapidly.

Autopsy reports confirm that Gloria Davy is the only one of the eight with signs of having been anally raped.

Then Speck pulls Davy on to the floor where Cora, only a few feet away, watches him stab and slice her to death.

Evidently Speck has lost count and forgotten about Cora.

When he's done with Gloria Davy and very bloody he goes into the bathroom and stays there a long time.

Finally Cora hears the toilet flush and sees Speck reappear still dripping with blood.

Through an ankle-high river of blood he shuffles toward the door and lets himself out.

Cora waits for two hours before she dares to come out from under the bed and call for help.

The manhunt commences.

Speck had homemade tats: **Love/Hate** on his left and right knuckles, and **Born to Lose** on his upper left arm.

He did the last one after smelling then finding Glenda and Barney the giant conjugating on the floor.

Speck spends what's left of the night at the Star, a South Side flophouse.

The next a.m. he is back at Skuggs, drinking.

Amazingly, he has brought the 12-inch butcher knife that he used to slice and dice eight nurses.

He's scrubbed most but not all of the blood off it.

He displays the knife to Sven the bartender.

After his tenth or twelfth Jim Beam Coke, Speck suddenly grabs Sven from behind and holds the butcher knife to his throat.

"This yere's how I'd keal yuh if I had tuh," Speck spits into Sven's ear, then lets him go.

Sven—all nerves—backs up behind the bar and waves a baseball bat.

Orders Speck out of Skuggs.

Speck, grinning, tosses some bills on the bar, fits the long knife under his jacket, leaves.

He goes into a nearby bar called Top Hat and resumes drinking.

When he stumbles, drunk, out of Top Hat at 9:25 p.m., he sees his face plastered on wanted posters and in the tabloids.

Back at the Star, Speck tries to kill himself by slashing his wrists. Only he messes up and passes out.

He is transported in an ambulance to the Emergency Room of the South Chicago Community Hospital.

The same hospital where the murdered nurses were attached.

Once in the ER, a Filipina aide spots his tats and notifies the police.

Tried in 1967, Speck is sentenced to die.

He appeals and is re-sentenced to 400 years in Stateville Correctional Center, a maximum-security prison in Joliet.

He's cited as a suspect in the disappearance and/or murder of five more women between May to July 1966, but is never charged.

He dies in 1991 of a heart attack at the age of 48, still behind bars.

In May, 1996, Richard Speck comes back to life in a pornographic video made secretly in prison.

The tape, thought to have been shot in 1988, shows a bloated Speck with a blonde bobbed wig, hormone-enhanced tits, wearing woman's red silk panties, casually snorting from a huge pile of coke, rolling joints, going down on his black "bitch," and bragging about how many times he's been fucked in the ass.

Turning to the camera he smirks "If yawl on'y knew how much fun I'se havin' in Stateville, yawl'd tun me loose."

Nobody seems to know who made the video or how.

At one point in the video Speck casually admits to having murdered the eight nurses, then shrugs, and says:

"Reckon it just wasn't their night."

Stateville Correctional Center is considered one of the harshest state prisons in the country.

It was the setting for the riot scene in Oliver Stone's mega-grossing *Natural Born Killers.*

● Carlos the Jackal ●

Portly and graying in a cream polo shirt and wine-red ascot, he sauntered into the courtroom looking more like an aging Latin lounge singer than the most notorious international terrorist since Che Guevara.

But Carlos the Jackal quickly dispelled any doubts about his revolutionary zeal.

"My profession is professional revolutionary," he asserted in his raspy tenor.

"My domain is the world.

"My mission is to transform your dreams into nightmares."

Why do you say that about nightmares and such? What do you have against ordinary people, Carlos?

It's on behalf of ordinary people that I say it.

It was only now at the start of his trial for the 1975 killing of two French intelligence agents and a Lebanese comrade, that the public has had a close-up look at the man, who, while eluding authorities for decades and carrying out attacks that by some estimates left 123 dead and countless numbers discomfited, existed only in grainy black and white photographs.

The insouciant, overweight terrorist acknowledged that his given name was Ilyich Ramirez Sanchez.

How did you get that weird name, Ilyich?

My parents were Communists. They admired Vladimir Ilyich

Lenin. I have a brother named Lenin and another named Vladimir. ***Helluva name for a Venezuelan kid to be saddled with. Ilyich.***

Carlos the Jackal gained his international notoriety as the Cold War-era mastermind of deadly bombings, assassinations, and hostage dramas.

He was reputed to have conceived the 1975 seizure of OPEC oil ministers, and he was involved in the 1976 Palestinian hijacking of a French jetliner to Entebbe, Uganda,

Which climaxed with the celebrated Israeli commando raid.

Subsequently turned into an award-winning motion picture produced and directed by Spielberg, I believe.

In the process Carlos the Jackal got to rub elbows with the ruthless Ugandan dictator and prodigious sex maestro Idi Amin.

Is it true what they say about Idi Amin?
What who says?
Six-feet-seven, 340 pounds, and hung like a Brahma bull in stud? The only tyrant who's supposed to come close to him—and he's at least a few light years behind—is Castro of Cuba.

Early in his career, Carlos the Jackal was also linked to the 1972 massacre of 11 Israeli athletes at the Munich Olympics.

Though Mossad, the Israeli secret service, later reported that it was Gaddafi, the Libyan warlord, and not Carlos the Jackal who was involved.

Like Carlos the Jackal, Idi Amin, and Castro of Cuba, the outlandishly costumed Gaddafi fancied himself a sex virtuoso, with however the crucial distinction of being radically under-endowed.

According to Mossad.

After eluding capture for decades, Carlos the Jackal is being tried for the Paris killings of two French investigators and an athletic Arab, formerly a comrade in the Popular Front for the Liberation of

Palestine, who the Jackal suspected was an informer.

With thinning hair and greying mustache, the paunchy Venezuelan once known as a ladies' man pranced, preened and beamed at the six women in the nine-member jury as they took their places, drawing muffled laughter from the standing-room audience.

According to the prosecutor, a razor-thin, sallow-visaged bachelor named Yves-Alain Chabrol, the Jackal "had a very utilitarian concept of sex, namely to seduce those creatures who could serve him in his terrorist projects."

You have been portrayed as a fat child who was desperate for attention. Is it true that fellow students in Venezuela called you "El Gordo," the fat one?

I didn't go to school in Venezuela. I went to public school in London then to Patrice Lumumba University in Moscow.

One theory is that your relentless sexual predation was an overcompensation for your obesity.

I was fat and I'm still somewhat fat. That's all there is to it.

Is it true that you bedded more than seventeen hundred females in your time?

My time is now. I'm not yet erased. History is still being constructed.

So you expect to somehow get out of prison and continue your philandering.

I expect to infect your dreams tonight.

Not me. I surf the Net. I play and romp on my website. But I never, ever dream.

Carlos the Jackal faces 30-year prison terms for each of the three killings.

He was convicted in absentia in 1992, but French law requires a retrial when and if the defendant is physically present.

Repeatedly describing himself as a "professional revolutionary in the Leninist tradition," Carlos the Jackal insisted he was fighting "for humanity, for the people of Palestine," and against "the McDonald–ization of civilization," allegedly propagated by "barbaric America and Zionist state terrorism."

You have been called an anti-Semite. Is that a fair characterization?
Aren't Palestinians Semites?
You tell me.
If I tell you you will distort it or forget it.

French sharpshooters were deployed around the courthouse for the weeklong trial and all entrances were equipped with body scanners.

Unlike the spectacular OJ Simpson trial in the US, *L'Affaire de Jackal* was neither being televised nor reported on the Internet,

Which, American experts say, is an expression of France's unremitting hostility to high technology,

Which France rather simplistically identifies with the United States,

With whom France has had a hate-love affair since the US liberated them from the Nazis,

With whom the French—not known for their moral stamina—were conveniently playing footsie.

The jurors, their alternates, and the three judges were each appointed two bodyguards, a chauffeur, and a bulletproof Citroën sedan.

Extravagant protection from an absurdly narcissistic, grossly overweight, revolution-spouting gasbag at the end of his tether.

Once known as a crack marksman with a flair for Latin dancing and seduction,

Coddled son of a wealthy Communist lawyer-father and opera-singer mother,

Aficionado of vintage French wines and Havana cigars,

As proud of his delicate hands and feet as of his idealization of the colonized and oppressed,

Carlos the Jackal was, indisputably, the international terrorist superstar par excellence.

The Jackal fell hard after French agents captured him in Khartoum, Sudan.

(With the complicity of Sudanese leftists).

Drugged him, dumped him in a body bag, and spirited him to Paris, depositing him in solitary confinement in a high-security detention center north of the city.

It's been reported that you were especially close to your mother, Kirsten, the opera singer.

She was a cabaret, not an opera singer. Her name was Concepción.

Sorry. I confused your diskette with Danny the Red's. The overweight Maoist terrorist. Who despised Germany as much as you despise the US. Concepción, your mother, modeled herself on Marlene Dietrich, didn't she? The whole bisexual thing. Was that an influence on your own sexuality, which reputedly was not strictly limited to females?

Carlos the Jackal lived behind the Iron Curtain, hence beyond the grasp of Western governments, for years.

But life on the lam became increasingly onerous.

With the fall of the Berlin Wall in 1989, his East Bloc protectors faded into the masonry.

Which coincided with the already-corpulent Jackal putting on weight, especially around the hips and buttocks.

And with his once theatrical blue-black Latin hair falling out in clumps.

When his main Middle Eastern protectors no longer had any use for him, the Frogs made their move.

Carlos the Jackal, who speaks Spanish, Russian, Arabic, and halting French, has spent his time behind bars boning up on French law and studying the language in preparation for the trial.

French legal procedures are complex and time-consuming.

And if you are not fluent in their fetishized language you might as well throw in the towel.

Have you made satisfactory progress with your studying of French law?

I'd make better progress if they supplied me with the texts I've requested.

For a reputed cocksman like you the enforced celibacy must be a considerable sacrifice.

I've made sacrifices for thirty years. That's what it means to be a professional revolutionary.

Flashback to June 27, 1975.

Ilyich Ramirez Sanchez was posing as a lumpy 26-year-old mathematics student in a tiny Latin Quarter flat in a side street near the Sorbonne, when two unarmed investigators knocked.

Raymond Queneau and Jean-Luc Gabin, of the Direction de la Sécurité du Territoire, France's FBI, were investigating an attack on Israel's El Al airlines at Paris' Orly Airport in January of that year.

Queneau was slight and sly like a ferret, whereas Gabin was large and gruff like a bear.

Accompanying the two investigators to 11 Toulier St., Arrondisement 5, was Muammar Moukharbal, a fellow militant-turned-informer from the Popular Front for the Liberation of Palestine, who had been apprehended earlier that month.

Moukharbal (Lebanese) bore an uncanny resemblance to the youthful Omar Sharif (Egyptian).

Even to having a sexy gap between his top two front teeth.

However he walked springily on the balls on his feet like Sean Connery as 007.

As the mustached Moukharbal raised his right hand and pointed to Carlos the Jackal, the Jackal pulled out an UZI machine pistol and opened fire, killing the rangy Arab and the two Sécurité agents on the spot.

He then fled Gaul.

Hating Israelis doesn't prevent you from using their UZI machine pistol.

I use whatever technology works most effectively. Nor do I feel enmity towards individual Israelis.

Carlos the Jackal's fingerprints on the UZI and his own later description of the killings have given the prosecution a seemingly airtight case.

But these being the French, anything is possible.

In 1979, the pan-Arab newspaper, *Asharq al Awsat*, published an interview, purportedly with Carlos the Jackal, in which he acknowledged killing Muammar Moukharbal as a "traitor to the cause of the people."

Carlos the Jackal has since denied giving the interview and claims he was framed by Mossad and French police agents, who, at the instigation of the US, wanted to create a rift between France and the Palestinian cause.

"It wasn't an interview but an article," the Jackal insisted.

"The author wasn't a journalist but a poet.

"Moreover she was in love with me.

"She portrayed me as she imagined me."

The Soviet Union had expelled Carlos the Jackal as a troublemaker in 1970 when he and his twin brother, Lenin, were reportedly spending more time partying than studying at Patrice Lumumba University in Moscow.

According to the documents, Carlos the Jackal and Lenin persisted in drinking enormous quantities of tequila rather than Russian-produced vodka.

Which didn't exactly endear them to their rabidly nationalist hosts.

In his defense the Jackal claimed in his memoirs that he had nothing against vodka, but didn't want to get poisoned from the radiation that leached into the grain used to produce the vodka after Chernobyl.

Fair enough, except that the Chernobyl nuclear power plant disaster occurred sixteen years later, in 1986.

Patrice Lumumba. Was he the one they murdered in South Africa?

That was Steve Biko. They murdered Lumumba in the Congo.

Are you and Lenin identical twins?

Yes. Only he wears a vandyke like his namesake. As you see, I have just the mustache.

Carlos, I'd like to propose an exercise. I say a name and you say immediately what pops into your skull. Agreed?

Do I have a choice?

No. Here we go. Evita Peron?

G-spot squirting.

Che?

G-spot squirting.

You already said that. I'll repeat: Che?

Antihistamine.

The Kennedy clan?

No prepuce.

Mother Teresa?

Piss Christ.

Chairman Arafat?

Funky curry.

Madonna?

Henry Kissinger.

Is it true that you had a sexual liaison with Madonna? Idi Amin fore and you aft? Maybe it was the other way around. It was DP in any case. According to Mossad. Double penetration. By two of the fattest-assed terrorists in Christendom. Was she as good as advertised? Madonna?

After his rejection by the Soviet Union and the Arab states, first the corrupt Communist secret police of East Germany then Bulgaria harbored Carlos the Jackal in the mid-to-late 1980s.

Keeping a wary eye on his activities on their soil.

But evidently not worrying much about his depredations in other venues, which at that juncture included the horn of Africa, southeast Asia, Central America, and the Caribbean.

It remained to be seen whether Carlos the Jackal would win over the jury with his rambling answers mixed with bravura, flirtation, and sloganeering in his bumbling French.

A former mistress-turned informer, Dominique Sanda, reportedly a post-op M2F transsexual who lives on the formerly chic isle of Ibiza, was expected to testify for the prosecution when the trial resumed today.

Carlos, have you ever had the sense of an infinitely tender, infinitely merciful entity circulating around and through us day and night?
Now that you mention it.
To my way of thinking, it's the Godhead, or the head of God.
To my way of thinking, it's Vladimir Ilyich Lenin, at the Revolution's deepest penetration, his eyes on fire, his pantaloons bulging at the crotch, his vandyke razor-sharp, grey but not yet white.

Postscript: The unrepentant revolutionary terrorist known as Carlos the Jackal was, today, sentenced to life in prison for the killing of three souls on the left bank of Paris in 1975.

Carlos the Jackal's response before being shackled and led away?
"Viva la revolución!"

However several in attendance disputed this. According to them, Carlos the Jackal's final words were "*Allahu akbar!*", the terrorist Islamic slogan which means "God is great."

⊕ Manson ⊖

Even the Devil—If there is a Devil—Had a Beginning

Dr. Pepper

My ma's younger brother was named Luther Kinlock. He lived in West Virginia, which is where we moved from Ohio when I was not even a year old. Luther didn't have no kind of real job so him and Kathleen—my ma—they decided to rob a gas station in Charleston, West Virginia. What they used as a weapon was a full bottle of Dr. Pepper which they tried to hit the attendant on the head with, but they messed up and got nabbed.

First rape

Bennett Home for Boys. Clarksburg, West Virginia. I was ten years old, the youngest, smallest kid in the joint. Seven, eight bigger kids—they gang-raped me. When I got it together to go to the assistant superintendent, mo'fucker called Fish, he told me pull my pants down, bend over and show where they got me. When I did he spit tobacco juice on his hand and shoved it up my ass. Then he says to the guard: "Okay, he's primed, let them fuck his brains out."

I never got a chance to even things up with Fish, but that night at about three a.m. I took a window crank—one of them steel rods that push open or pull shut the windows. Was about sixteen inches long and about three pounds. I went to the bunk of the first dude that fucked my ass and hit him eight or nine blows hard as I could hit to the head and face. About killed him. Too fuckin' bad I dint.

Father Flanagan's Boys Town

They sent my ass there after I busted out of Bennett. But I busted out of Flanagan after like four days, me and some other kids. Stole cars and broke into stores an' shit. Even held up one old guy and slapped him around a little bit. They caught us four days later. Sent me to Prideaux Juvenile Detention in Indiana, which was raunchy. But I wasn't 'bout to do no time at no Father Motherfucker's Boys Town.

Pelican Bay

Where I'm at now? Ain' no biggie. Tomorrow—if I'm alive—they could transfer me to some other hard-ass joint, you dig? How many state and federal joints I been in my life, dog? Ain' nothin' changed. No, no, no, no. Negativity, man. If I ask for a bucket of shit they're like: No fuckin' way, Manson.

Truth is they'd ruther see me dead. 'Cept they afraid the fuckin' consequence. Still folks out there love my ass. If they don't love me, they need me, you dig? Most the other big-time devil soundbites are dead and gone: Hitler, Nixon, Bundy, John Wayne Gacy, Che Guevara.

Me, I'm at world's end, shackled, sensory deprived, under 24/7 surveillance, but I'm Charles mo'fuckin' Manson, evil incarnate, you dig?

Death Valley

I dreamt of the desert but never seen it till, what?, '67. Was love at first sight, dog. Plus I'm a quick study. If I wasn't I wouldna made it this far.

Coyote

Jesus crucified. You ever see a coyote move? He's rhythm and grace. He's aware of everything that's in motion because it's either prey or something gonna prey on him. You listen close for a long time to the coyote and you gonna hear just about every sound there is—howl, bark, growl, yip, wail, whistle. The coyote is total fear, total paranoia, which is what you must have to survive on this fucked-over planet. Yet he's relaxed, delicate in all his movements, at peace in his total fear that never ends. If a coyote is ever in trouble or captured he will do whatever it takes to get free, bite off his own tail or leg, even change identities, like become a sidewinder or a crow. That's why the Indians call him Trickster. If I was an animal I'd be a coyote. If I wasn't a coyote I'd be a scorpion.

Rommel in the desert

Yeah, I was gonna have my tribe raid some the neighboring towns, turn all them born-agains into anti-capitalist hippies.

Rommel in the desert, Buddha in the desert, Jesus in the desert. I had all kinds of shit in mind one time or 'nother. You drop acid a bunch your mind gets to zoomin'. Mostly, I just wanted to be left alone with my coyotes and scorpions and geetar. I never made no big deal out of it. I was livin' in the desert. You all done come and git me, remember? I was happy doin' what I'm doin'.

Assistant DA Bugliosi

Dude wanted to gas as much of the Manson family as he could get his hands on, you dig? He'd be right there in the execution chamber, first row, jackin' off in his head.

There I was on Death Row in Quentin kinda looking forward to the gas. But after that ACLU challenge went to the Supreme Court they postponed then commuted all the pending executions. Had nothing to do with compassion, you dig? Was a legal thing. This country of yours ain' into no compassion for po' folks.

Like I said, I didn't give a shit either way, but not executing Manson broke Bugliosi all up, I thought he was like to weep.

You got to understand that beneath Bugliosi's DA swagger he was a puss. In that lyin' book he got rich on, he has me so mojo powerful that just remembering one my stares would stop his pissing mid-flow.

The Manson stare

It's simple, basic voodoo. Like me starin' at you now. You see how I'm starin' at you? Answer me, dog.

I see

Cool. Now you go home and try to fuck your wife, you ain' gonna be able. Just lookin' at you I can see that your sex life wasn't worth shit to begin wit'. But I just wrecked what was left of it for all time.

Voodoo

Thas right. I'm in Pelican Bay State Penitentiary, 68-years-old, shackled, sensory deprived, under constant surveillance, but I'm Charley Manson, you dig. So folks send me stuff—presents, neckties, socks, sweaters. But I ain' no clothes horse and never was. Naked and dick swinging's my deal. So what I do with my hands cuffed is unravel the ties and socks and sweaters and tank tops 'n shit and make voodoo dolls. I make scorpions and cockroach cages too.

[laughs] My dolls done murdered and maimed some bad-ass human mo'fuckers. You know as well as me some folks ain' fit to live.

Manson orgies on video

[laughs] Yeah, we shot a lot of fim and vid. Plus other folks—visitors and such—they shot us. We looked good and we knew how to fuck and suck. Ever'body wanted a piece of us. Some the fims we ourselves took we swapped for dope. The other fims—I know where they're at, and they're hot.

Yo! dog, get my ass sprung from Pelican Bay and I'll make sure you be doin' a whole lot of jackin' off to Manson and his family.

God of fuck

Got Bugliosi all worked up. That's 'cuz he's a tight-ass career-sucking opportunist that don't even know what it means to fuck. I said I was the god of fuck to Lynette Squeaky Fromme first time I done her. Underneath a great old Redwood. Go ask Squeaky how she liked it. Go ask all my other sweet-smelling girls. They was sweet-smelling back then. Cain't say how they smell now the Law has got in their panties.

Sadie Mae Glutz

Shot off her mouth in jail. Sold some made-up story to one of the weeklies. Copped a plea before the grand jury. Became a quote-unquote born-again. That's what she claimed anyway. Bought her some pity, but didn't get her ass sprung.

Before she joined up with the family she was a devil worshiper with what's his face up there in San Francisco. LaVey. Mindfuck was her thing. Whatever Sadie was into Sadie wanted to be top dog, you dig? Fucking included. With me that never happened, you dig? After I balled her inside out and sideways, she done cried like a little girl. She'd go on 'bout how I was God. Which is dog spelled backwards.

Like some people, they say Sadie's gorgeous and sexy. You know what? Even the bulldykes in Frontera, where she's at, they won't go near her. She's toxic. I never dug Sadie Mae Glutz, never trusted her even back when she called herself Susan Atkins. She even smelled raunchy. Her skin, her hair.

Kashmir Clap

[laughs] That's a Sadie deal, right? If Sadie caught the clap she done caught it outside the family. She'd spread for anything that farted.

How many young folks moving through the family did I fuck? Eight hundred? Thousand? Not a one of 'em ever had the Kashmir clap or the Timbuktu clap to my knowledge. And I reckon I'd be the mo'fucker to know.

Nature lover, vegetarian

That's me. Just like Gandhi.

Just like Hitler

I ain' got nuffin' 'gainst Hitler, dog. Hitler's coo'. Monster like me. That's what yawl made me. You fear me and you want to fuck me. Ain't that why you got all hotted up about the fims was shot of the family orgies?

Where are the films at, Charlie? How can I get my doggy paws on 'em? How can I slobber all over them with my forked tongue?

Haight-Ashbury

It's 1967 and I just finished up a 15-year deal at Terminal Island, a fed joint near San Pedro. I told 'em I didn't want to leave and they laughed at me. Bunch of murders and mayhem later *[laughs]*, they wish they done kept my ass inside.

Takes me a little while get my shit together, then I go up to the Haight because I hear that's where the cool runnings is at. I play my geetar, right? The fems just keep comin'. Mary Brunner—she was a librarian at the University of San Francisco medical school. I was pickin' on the street near Golden Gate Park, my black watch cap on the pavement for spare change. I see Mary Brunner walking her boxer, dog shit bag in her hand, nose in the air, and I say real soft, "Babe, listen to this yere melody. I play it just for you." She stopped, I played the song. Bang.

Mary was the first of the so-called Manson family. I called her Mercy and gave her the color blue. Then came Squeaky, which is what we called Lynette Fromme. I gave her the color green. Then came fucked-up Susan Atkins. Then Katie Krenwinkle, and Simi Valley Sheri. And Sandy Good.

It was getting crowded, you dig, so I scammed a school bus, painted it black. We rode from the Haight up and down the coast, into Utah, Nevada, then back down to LA, pickin' up girls at ever' stop. Once in a while there'd be a dude.

Manson does dudes?

Sho. I'm 68 years old and been in prison 56 years. Ain' no girls in prison that I know of.

ANDERSEN'S FAIRY TALES. 39

recognized her, although she had grown so tall and beautiful. "... others," said the eldest, "fly out ... swan so long as the sun is ... the sky, ... soon as it sink ... the hills, we ... over our ... shape. ... no dwell here, but ... and ... beyond the ... in. We are permitted to visit ... home ... ce ev ... to remain eleven. ... brown ... and we ... ba ... and ... for a whole year." ... Take ... with you, begged E ... the whole night, wea ... g a strong ... of rushes. In the ... E ... za placed herself ... in it ... the swan ... in their beak ... away they flew, till

do not dwell here

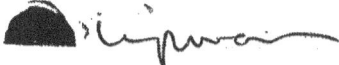

Was one male, pastor father of Ruth Ann Moorehouse. Ouisch we called her. She was like 14 when she got on the Manson bus outside of Flagstaff, I think it was. Man, could she fuck. Well, by the time we got to LA her old man—Pentecostal pastor from Broken Arrow, Oklahoma, where Ouisch run away from—was waitin' on me with another dude, great big shaved-head mo'fucker packin' a semi-automatic. Desert Eagle 10 mm, if I remember correct.

No biggie. Problem solving is what I excel at, you dig? I sweet-talked them a little, fixed the shaved-head loon up with two my girls, then took a private walk with the preacher, slipped him some acid, and fucked him in the ass. You know that these Pentecostals talk in tongues, right? Well, this dude, Ouisch's old man out of Broken Arrow, Oklahoma, was squealin' in tongues while I was punkin' him. That's how much he loved my dick in his ass, you dig?

I dint feel the same way. Was like stickin' my fist in a sewer drain. After that, "Preacher" was one my most loyal followers. Till he died a year or so later.

Submit

You and honkies like you cain't see that these hundreds of young humans that joined my family were humans that you all abandoned, humans alongside the road that, when they wouldn't eat their cheese-burgers, their parents kicked them out or tried to stick them in Juvenile Hall. So I done the Christian thing and took them in and told them that in love there was no wrong. All they had to do was give up the lies and bad shit they learned and submit. Submission.

Did I submit my own self? Damn right. You can't enjoy fucking or even getting stoned if you don't submit.

Anger and rage

My ma dropped me when she was 16 and a ho cuz she was an illiterate Appalachian hillbilly. I never knew my father. We scrambled from town to town. I done 7 years for a 37 dollar check. I done 12 years because I was piss-poor without no parents. I was gang-raped in reform school when I was ten years old. Yeah, dog, I had anger and rage.

How's anyone not going to have anger and rage living in what they done turned this sweet world into?

Mystical hole in Death Valley

What was down the hole it ain' for honkies like you all to know. But I'll say this. I found a hole that goes down to a river that runs north underground. I called it a bottomless pit because where could a river be flowing north underground? Was so wide and deep you could even sail a ship on it. Was no penal institutions and TV down there. So I covered it up and called it "The Devil's Hole," and we all laughed and joked about it.

Black folks

Ever since I shot that big wannabe Black Panther spade Lotsapoppa in '69, I think it was, people, even so-called Manson experts, been sayin' I have trouble with blacks and such, but it ain' no truth to it. Lotsapoppa ripped me off in a drug deal. He coulda been French or Chinese and I still woulda shot his ass. Black dint have noth-in' to do with it.

Like Lamar Duane Cady, we called him Fang, the Skull Helmet biker that lived on the movie ranch, he hated blacks, and when he'd rap with me I'd like nod my head. So he'd go away sayin': Charlie agrees with me. But I was just reflectin' back what he hisself thought.

Yo, I been in prison all my life, and that's the first thing you learn: go wit' the flow 'less you're big enough and shit-eating enough to bust some heads. See, I ain' big, but I'm shit-eating.

You know what else I am? I'm a piss-poor hillbilly spend all my fuckin' life in prison. Prisons in damn near ever' city in this country of yours. And who's in these prisons of yours? Black folks and po' folks. A piss-poor hillbilly in the joint ain' nuffin' but a nigger.

Reflecting back

What I'm reflectin' back is this yere country we live in. Hypocrisy, lust in the head, xenophobia, cruelty to your brother. It ain't that I am or do these things, you dig, but that people—Christian family people like you all—see in me what's in their deepest selves but that they cain't bear to look at. That's why for so long I was the most famous face in all of capitalism.

Pimp Manson

Thas me. I was into a bunch of shit, you dig. And, yeah, pimpin' was one my thangs. An older con that ran with Bonnie and Clyde—he told me once there was nothing like turning a chick out. He was on the money, dog. Deep down every fem wants to be a ho. I was real good at seeing they got what they wanted. And it bought me time to set around, get stoned, do my music.

Punked in Quentin

'Nother lie makin' the rounds, that some Aryan Brotherhood dude made me his bitch when I was in Quentin in the early Seventies. Nobody done touched me inside since that time I was gang-raped as a kid. Well, this Pachuco gang doused me with paint thinner and lit me up. That was in Calipatria, by the border. I got some my hair and skin burned. No big deal. And three skanky Hare Krishna cons jumped me, but that was in Soledad. Anyway I kicked their asses all over the yard, the three of 'em.

The Krishnas thought I was dissing their Hindu jive. With the Mex gang it was Macho shit. I was a big target, okay? Light Manson up and get famous. Gonna take a lot more than Pachuco punks and skanky Krishnas to do me any real hurt.

Cocksman

[laughs] Yo lookin' at him.
Lotta folks ask me who was better, me or Cupid, Bobby

Beausoleil. Lovin' good takes a good dick, but that ain' all. It's like the way innocent little kids play, every bit of the body alive. Me, I fired from all cylinders. At the same time I always took my time, knew just what the fem wanted. And I gave it to her. Just not all at once, you dig?

Yeah, the family girls loved Cupid's dick, and he knew how to use it. But after I copped him in the ass I owned him. He'd do anything I say.

Roman Polanski

A kind of ham. Polish ham.

Dennis Wilson of the Beach Boys

I was waitin' on him at his mansion, it was like 2:30 a.m. As he pulled into the fancy driveway in his purple Ferrari I stepped out of the shadows. Dude saw me and was like: Please don't hurt me. I said: Do I look like I'm going to hurt you, brother? And I never did hurt him. Though sometimes he gave me cause. He copped my music, you know, stuck it on one of his LP's, changed a few my lyrics and never gave me no credit for it.

Two-and-a-half incandescent years

I know where you're goin', dog, 'cuz other people—so-called Manson experts—come up with the exact same thing. The whole Manson family deal was between May '67 and December '69. We done a lifetime load of bad shit during that real short time.

So if I was offered a devil's bargain: two-and-a-half years, like what I had with my girls and sex and dope and Death Valley and those raunchy murders that I supposedly done or instigated—if I was offered them two-and-a-half years in exchange for spending the rest of my life in prison, would I take it?

You know what, dog, it took me a while to get in the groove. After doin' 15 years in Terminal Island I was on the streets a lot of days before I got my nuts out of hock. Once I found the groove, though, it done never stopped. And I ain' gonna lie to you: I enjoyed the ride.

'Cept close to the end, around the time the big murders—'cuz there was some other murders folks still don't know about—close to the end, the shit turned. Was me callin' the shots and I let us slip into this end-of-the-world thing, diggin' up bunkers, storing water and supplies, keepin' a step ahead of the pigs that was out to nail us. All that Helter Skelter shit.

Family would look at me like, "What now, Charlie?" And I wasn't always able to tell' 'em. My creativity was like slipping. I guess it was that two-and-a-half year devil's pact comin' to an end.

But would I do it again, even if I knew on one side was prison and on the other side was prison? Yeah, I would. Because prison ain' that big a deal, dog. Jail sucks but it's my life.

Helter Skelter

Was a goof. Bunch of us on the movie ranch was stoned on acid and jivin' around. Someone, I think maybe Snake, come up with that Beatles White Album and we got to listenin' to it close, with the acid workin'. So we started messin' around with the "Revolution" lyrics an' shit. To DA Bugliosi, it was like: Revolution plus Beatles plus Manson = big time $$$ for his own self. So he ran wit' it. He's full of poop. I could care less about the fuckin' White Album. I'm a hillbilly. Gimme Woody Guthrie. Gimme Hank Williams senior. Gimme early Dylan on acoustic.

Sharon Tate murders

Wasn't me that murdered her, dog. I didn't know her or the Polish ham that was her husband cuz I never did see none their flicks. Yeah, I hung out a little with actors 'n shit, and this one famous matinee idol—he's dead now and I won't say his name—paid me to fuck his ass. But I never mixed with no Sharon Tate and Polish ham.

Freaky shit, I like it

Sadie Mae Glutz said that when she tasted the blood off the knife she used to stab Sharon Tate in her pregnant belly. Sadie admitted it then denied it. But Tex Watson and Katy Krenwinkle both heard her say it.

Jesus

You a church-going dog so maybe you know that before the church fathers got ahold of him, Jesus was an Essene, a hippy. He wore a jellaba, which is a long robe, with no underwear, not even a jock strap. What a family man like you would call an athletic supporter. He had long hair, and traveled with a bunch of long-haired followers. Apostles he called them. Ring a bell?

Manson of a thousand faces

You five-foot-three and in hard-ass penal institutions your whole damn life you learn to adjust or else you die. You puff up like Mike Tyson, you vibe out like Jesus, you squeeze and shrink and fade like road kill…

You a dog and a foo', but you got to understand just a little bit of this without my sayin'. Man, I sometimes wish they'd send me someone has some brain and maybe just a little bit of soul. But I reckon ain' too many like that out there. See, what you and your kind are is just what we was fightin' 'gainst back then. Rid the fuckin' earth of yawl.

You lost that fight

Wrong again. What you all think is lost has just gone underground. Like a desert plant, you dig? Could take another ten, twenty years for the right conditions then it will rise again faster than you can believe, all strong and prickly. Foo' like you put his hand on it come away poisoned and bloody.

Favorite mass-murderer excluding yourself

Finally you come up wit a question that ain' half-ass. Favorite

mass-murderer excluding myse'f?

That would be Henry Kissinger. Madonna called him Caca. She was fuckin' him. You remember OJ, right? The Juice? Well, OJ'd bang Madonna from behind while she doin' a strap-on number on Caca. Sometimes she'd ram her fist up there. He liked it, Caca. His stretch limo would be waitin' outside Madonna's Park Avenue triplex. Was a regular occurrence, Madonna, OJ, Caca. This was way before the OJ trial.

OJ's guy, Johnny Cochran

Uh-huh. I sometimes think what if I had slick Johnny Cochran argue my case. Know what? I woulda fuckin' walked. I'd be back in the desert with the coyotes and scorpions fingerin' my geetar.

Provisional Final Words

Yo, I had my run. Two-and-a-half incandescent years. Ain't that the word you used: incandescent? Now I'm back inside where I belong. It's my home. Ever'body has to have some kinda home. Pelican Bay. Don't it have a nice sound? You know what I do in my solitary cell in Pelican Bay? I sit there thinking of nothing. Nothing to think about. If I could, I'd jerk this microphone out and beat your brains out with it, because that's what you and the rest yawl deserve. But I don't have none that anger and rage you was talkin' about. You're a scabby, housebroken old dog. A dumb, soulless mother-fuckin' piece of shit wears a nametag and do just what they want you to do. You know how quick I could slit your belly, snatch out your liver? But do I want to get your pissy blood all over me? No, I don't. I most definitely don't. I'm just sittin' here wit' my shackled hands pickin' my imaginary geetar waitin' on some ties and socks and tee shirts that I can make voodoo dolls out of for all them upstanding Christian human beans out there in Freedomland.

Notes

*Multiple texts, online and off, constitute much of the raw material that I've reimagined into my serial killer "docufictions." The Crime library, Melange, Angelfire, APBnews and individual killers' home-pages are among the Web sites I read or glanced over; as well as too many hard copy volumes to cite in this space.

**"Dr Death" was published in a somewhat different format in my volume *False Positive* (FC2, 2002).

Photo Courtesy Gayle Luque

Harold Jaffe is the author of eight fiction collections and three novels, including *False Positive* (2002), *Sex for the Millennium* (1999), *Othello Blues* (1996), Straight *Razor* (1995), *Eros Anti-Eros* (1990), *Madonna and Other Spectacles* (1988) and *Beasts* (1986). Jaffe's fiction has appeared in numerous journals and has been widely anthologized. His novels and stories have been translated into German, Japanese, Spanish, French, and Czech. Jaffe is editor-in-chief of Fiction International and Professor of Creative Writing and Literature at San Diego State.

www.ingramcontent.com/pod-product-compliance
Lightning Source LLC
Chambersburg PA
CBHW030144200626
46812CB00015B/1361